Biggles in Australia

Biggles in Australia

Captain W. E. Johns

Armada

First published in the U.K. in 1955 by
Hodder & Stoughton Ltd., London.
This edition was first published in Armada in 1970 by
Fontana Paperbacks, 14 St. James's Place,
London SW1A 1PS

This impression 1981

© The estate of the late W. E. Johns

Printed in Great Britain by
Love & Malcomson Ltd.,
Brighton Road, Redhill, Surrey.

CHAPTER I

A PRESSMAN SETS A POSER

When Biggles, in answer to a call on the intercom, entered the office of his chief, Air Commodore Raymond of the Special Air Section at Scotland Yard, he was greeted with a smile which he knew from experience was not prompted entirely by humour.

"I'm not much for betting, sir, but I'd risk a small wager that what you're going to tell me isn't really funny," he observed as he pulled up a chair.

"That would depend on how you looked at it," answered the Air Commodore drily. "Serious matters can sometimes provoke an ironical smile. Take a look at this. I thought you'd like to see it." He pushed across the desk a picture that had obviously been cut from a newspaper.

Biggles studied the photographic reproduction for some time without speaking and without a change of expression. It showed a group of seven men standing on a sandy beach with the sea in the background. The subjects were in tropical kit, creased, dirty, shrunken and generally disreputable. They were hatless, and all needed a hair-cut and a shave.

"Recognise anybody?" asked the Air Commodore, whimsically.

"Of course. Our old friend Erich von Stalhein, no less. He appears to have slipped into the soup—on this occasion without being pushed by me."

"Do you know any of the others?"

"I fancy I've seen one of them before, but not recently, and on the spur of the moment I can't place him. Where, may I ask, was this fascinating snapshot taken?"

"On the coast of north-west Australia."

Biggles's eyes opened wide. "*Australia!* For Pete's sake! Where will the ubiquitous Erich turn up next? What was he doing there?"

"That's what I'd like to know. At the time the photo was taken he had just come ashore."

"What did he *say* he was doing?"

"He said he was, or had been, studying oceanography."

Biggles smiled cynically. "Imagine von Stalhein sitting on the sea bed watching the winkles and things. How did this enchanting picture come into your hands?"

"It was spotted by Major Charles of Security Intelligence in a batch of newspapers just in from Australia. Actually, the picture was in several papers. He thought we might like to see it."

Biggles pushed the paper back across the desk. "You know, sir, von Stalhein is becoming a nuisance."

"I'd say he's a menace."

"Then why don't you do something about it?"

"I've told you before that we've no case against him; nor shall we have while he's clever enough to keep on the right side of the law."

"With the result that I spend half my time looking for him and the other half dodging him."

"Of course."

"What do you mean, of course?"

"While he's engaged in espionage, and you in counter-espionage, it's inevitable that you should always be bumping into each other—in the same way as in football the two centre-forwards are often in collision. He has to earn his living somehow and it's natural that he should stick to the job for which he was trained in one of the most efficient spy schools in the world—the Wilhelm-strasse. He's no more likely to settle down in a routine occupation than you are." The Air Commodore smiled. "Don't forget you must be as big a nuisance to him as he is to you."

Biggles nodded. "I suppose you're right. At least he keeps us busy and provides us with an excuse for staying in our jobs. How did this Australian affair come about?"

"Quite simply. A few weeks ago north-west Australia was visited by one of those devastating storms which we would call a hurricane but are known locally as willie-willies. They do immense damage, both at sea and ashore. After the one in question, three pearling luggers, out from Broome, failed to return to port, so aircraft of the Royal Australian Air Force were sent out to locate them, or possible survivors should they have been wrecked. One of the rescue aircraft spotted a ship's lifeboat, under sail, making for the mainland miles from anywhere—by which

I mean miles from the nearest point where food and water would be available. The pilot radioed the position, whereupon supplies were rushed to the spot where the boat was making its landfall. It seems that a newspaper reporter, scenting a story, also went along in a chartered plane, taking his camera. He got his story, such as it was, and, as you see, a photograph. In the matter of the picture a curious thing happened. At least, it struck the reporter as queer, and he referred to it in his article. When these shipwrecked mariners realised they had been photographed they kicked up a fuss and demanded that the film be destroyed."

"What reason did they give for that?"

"They said that as scientists they were opposed to any form of publicity."

"I bet they were," murmured Biggles, bitingly.

"Actually, that was a mistake, because, as I say, the reporter made a note of it, and certain sceptical editors, in their columns, asked for what possible reason these men should object to being photographed."

"We could tell them."

"Of course. Von Stalhein has good reasons for not wanting to see his face in any newspaper."

"What story did he tell. He'd have to offer some explanation."

"The spokesman of the party said they were a scientific expedition studying marine life in tropical waters. Their ship, the *See Taube*, out from Hamburg, was caught in the storm and cast ashore on an island. The seven were the sole survivors of a crew of twenty-two. The ship was pounded to pieces on a reef, but by good luck a lifeboat was washed up more or less intact. Having patched it up they set a course for the mainland. They had, of course, lost everything except the clothes they stood up in. Considering the state they were in their story was not questioned. We can assume that the shipwreck part of it was true."

"They would remember their names and nationalities—or did they lose those too?" inquired Biggles sarcastically.

"No. They gave their names. You'll find them in the paper. They were four Germans, two Poles, and a Britisher who said he was simply a member of the crew."

"Did von Stalhein's name appear among them?"

"No."

"That's what I thought. And I gather they could all speak English."

"So it seems."

"Very convenient, if they were going to land in Australia."

"They said they had no intention of landing in Australia—until they were cast away."

"Then the fact that they could all speak English must have been one of those curious coincidences we sometimes hear about," remarked Biggles, with a faint sneer of scepticism. "Where are they now?"

"No one knows, and, frankly, no one seems to care. They've just disappeared."

"How could they disappear?"

"They were flown to Darwin and provided with clothes and accommodation pending such time as arrangements could be made for them to return home. It seems that a few days later, an aircraft, chartered by a good Samaritan in the south, turned up and collected them. They just went; and as Darwin is an international port apparently the local people couldn't have cared less."

"Didn't this sudden departure strike anyone as odd?"

"Evidently not. Darwin is the sort of place where people come and go. After all, von Stalhein and his companions were not under any sort of suspicion. They were not being watched. They had broken no law. The police weren't interested in them. They were free to come and go as they wished."

"All nice and easy," muttered Biggles. "This good Samaritan, as you call him, must have been a contact man. No doubt he saw the picture in the papers, and realising what had happened, got busy. Which means, in plain English, there was already an enemy agent in Australia."

"That, as you would say, sticks out like a sore finger."

"Have you told Australia what we know von Stalhein to be?"

"Not yet."

"Why not?"

"I don't want to start a spy scare. At the moment von Stalhein is, I imagine, lying low, waiting to see what the outcome of this affair will be. If he decides that it has passed unnoticed by the Security people, both there and here, he may come into the open and proceed with what

8

he went to Australia to do. In which case we may catch up with him."

"Who do you mean by we?"

"Well—you."

Biggles reached for a cigarette. "Surely this is Australia's pigeon."

"Australia is part of the British Commonwealth, and as such it is also our pigeon. Of this we may be sure. If von Stalhein is in Australia he's not there for our good."

"I couldn't agree more. No doubt he and the rest of the party quietly faded away because they didn't want to be asked questions which might have been embarrassing. The point is, what questions were they asked when they were rescued. This island on which they were wrecked, for example. What's the name of it?"

"They didn't know."

"Stuff and nonsense! Of course they knew. Don't ask me to believe that the skipper of a vessel that size didn't know the position of his ship."

"What size?"

"With a ship's company of twenty-two it was obviously no mere cabin cruiser."

"There are plenty of islands off that particular coast."

"How long were they cast away on one."

"Three weeks—they said."

"If that's true we should have no great difficulty in finding it, because apart from the wreckage of the ship, seven men in three weeks would leave their mark. But that's a detail that can be gone into later—that's if you think this business is of such importance that it should be followed up."

"I certainly do."

"But you're not seriously expecting me to find von Stalhein in a place the size of Australia?"

"If we don't find the man we've got to know what he's doing. Apart from the fact that Australia is a fast-developing continent in which the Iron Curtain brigade would like to get their teeth, there are a lot of things going on there that they would like to know more about. No doubt they would like to have more information than we have released about the new rocket and guided missile ranges. They would like to know more about the present and future production prospects of the newly-discovered uranium deposits."

"They wouldn't need a ship for that."

"They'd need a ship to test the strength of any radio-activity persisting in the region of the Montebello Islands, where we exploded atomic bombs."

"You may have got something there," admitted Biggles. "Never mind what the ship was for, it was certainly needed or it wouldn't have been provided. In which case it would seem that an investigation into the purpose of enemy agents in Australia would have to cover not only the mainland but the hundreds of islands within striking distance of it."

"That, I'm afraid, is what it adds up to."

"I'm glad to hear you say you're afraid," said Biggles lugubriously. "You've good reason to be. So have I. You don't often hear me say that, but the prospect of finding a man, or even a small army of men, in a place the size of Australia, strikes me as having about as much hope of success as a boy looking for a lost peanut on a shingle beach on a dark night. I once had occasion to fly over a stretch of north-west Australia, and what I saw didn't make me pine to see more of it. I know it isn't all like that, but there's plenty that is.* No, sir. This isn't a job for one man. It'd be an undertaking for the entire Australian Police Force, and even then I wouldn't bet on them finding an elusive customer like dear Erich, who knows every trick of the game."

"The police are not likely to take kindly to the idea of looking for a man against whom there is no charge."

"They could deport him as an undesirable alien."

"That would only make matters worse. Even if he didn't slip back in he'd be replaced with someone else whom we don't even know. Better the devil you know than the devil you don't know is an old saying, and a true one. See what you can do. I'm not particularly interested in von Stalhein personally; but we must know what he and his party are doing. It's our job to find out. Knowing what we know we can't just let the thing slide."

Biggles shrugged. "Very well, sir. You win. I'll do my best to get a line but it's likely to be a slow business."

"Can I help in any way?"

Biggles thought for a moment. "You can let me have
* See *Biggles Works It Out.*

the name of the reporter who took that photo, the name of the pilot who sent out the S.O.S., and the pinpoint he gave on first spotting the boat at sea. That's where I shall start. It's the only place I can start. If, too, you can identify the aircraft that collected von Stalhein and his party at Darwin it may save me some time there. The control tower should know. It would be something if we knew where that machine came from, who hired it, and where it went. It might also be helpful if you could let me have the name and address of an Australian Security Officer with whom I could get in touch should the need arise."

"I'll attend to that. Anything else?"

"That's all I can think of at the moment, sir. I'll press on and get ready. It looks as if I shall need two machines, one for marine work and the other for overland. But we can talk about that later." Biggles got up.

"Australians are a hospitable lot so you might be going to a worse place," remarked the Air Commodore comfortingly.

"Then don't be surprised if you hear I've packed up chasing myself round the globe and gone in for sheep raising or something," was Biggles's last word as he went out.

Returning to the Operations Room he passed on the latest intelligence to his team of pilots.

"What's your own idea of this business," asked Algy, when he had finished.

"I haven't one," admitted Biggles. "Von Stalhein could be engaged on one or more of a dozen shady undertakings —all with an espionage background, of course. We can, however, be reasonably sure of one or two things. He was given a definite assignment, and an important one covering a wide field, or he would be working on his own instead of with a party. It involved, at any rate in the first place, marine work—unless the ship was provided to enable the party to get ashore without passing through a normal port of entry, as would be necessary if they were carrying equipment that would be questioned by the Customs officers."

"Are we sure they had a ship," put in Ginger.

"Yes. They wouldn't be likely to start from Europe in a rowing boat. They admitted a crew of twenty-two men. Why did they volunteer that information? I'd say because they knew that the story was more likely to be believed than if they had said they were in those dangerous waters in a small craft. Ships are expensive things, so behind von Stalhein there must be big money; which suggest a foreign government. The ship was the *See Taube*—Sea Pigeon. It came from Hamburg so we can check up on that. The rescue people didn't question it. That's understandable. The first thing they would do would be to get the castaways to civilisation, leaving the questions till later; but by that time, the party, as we know, had disappeared."

Bertie interposed. "But look here, old boy. If the blighters lost their ship they must have lost their gear, if any."

"That's what I'm hoping happened," answered Biggles. "If the ship broke up, and I think it must have done considering the plight the survivors were in, some of it, or some of the stuff it carried, might have been cast ashore. Working on that assumption I shall start by looking for the island."

"How many islands are there to be searched," asked Ginger.

"I don't know," replied Biggles. "We shall know more about that when we've studied the chart. Speaking from memory there are quite a lot; but that needn't worry us unduly, because the one with which we're concerned can't be any great distance from the spot where the lifeboat was first seen. As the pilot of the aircraft pinpointed the position it will be on record."

"This seems to be a more hopeless job than most of those that come our way," remarked Algy.

"That's what I told the chief. But he argued that it wasn't as sticky as all that because although Australia is a big slice of land there's a limit to the number of places in which von Stalhein would be interested. I hope he's right. But we'd better see about getting organised. We shall need a land plane with plenty of endurance, which means the Halifax; but I've no intention of cruising around the Timor Sea in something that'll sink if we get ditched. I'll take Ginger with me in the Sea Otter we used on that West Indian Job.* I'd take the Sunderland but there might be difficulties in refuelling. From that angle an amphibian would be safer. Algy, you and Bertie can trundle out to Darwin in the Halifax. We'll travel independently and meet there. Now let's have a look at the chart and see

* See *Biggles In The Blue*.

12

where we're going. When I say going I'm thinking particularly of where we're going to park the machines. There's no dearth of aerodromes, even if they're a long way apart; but except for refuelling I shall endeavour to keep clear of them, for if ever it reaches von Stalhein's ears that we're in Australia he'll know why, and our job will be even more difficult than it is now. And while I think of it, as we're talking about moorings, never forget that on the north-west coast of Australia the difference between high water and low can be up to nearly forty feet. So watch your tides. Now let's look at the map."

CHAPTER II

WIDE OPEN SPACES

THE arrangements made by Biggles for his Australian assignment were rather more involved than usual on account of the peculiar conditions in which they would have to operate. Where the quest would eventually lead them was an unknown quantity, and, as he told the others, it was as well to be prepared for anything. They were going to a continent, not a country, and while it was now well provided with aerodromes the distances between them was a factor that would have to be considered in conjunction with refuelling. They didn't want to spend half their time flying to distant points for fuel and oil, much of which would be exhausted on the return journey, thus hampering their mobility and putting them in a constant state of anxiety.

The matter was complicated by the employment of a marine aircraft, although the machine, a Sea Otter, being an amphibian, could operate from both land or water. The Otter was an ideal craft for investigating the islands, and it would be able to refuel at the several landing grounds strung out along the coast between Perth and Darwin; but it hadn't the endurance range of the Halifax, with its special tanks, which would in many ways be more suitable for long-distance overland flights.

Biggles admitted that this question of refuelling worried

13

him, because people would wonder what they were doing and perhaps ask questions. Word of them might be carried by the regular air line pilots to the cities on which they were based, and so reach the ears of von Stalhein or his confederates, who might be anywhere. In order to avoid being seen too often, should the exploration of the islands turn out to be a long business, Biggles had an idea of using the Halifax as a refuelling tender. Working from Port Darwin, it should, he thought, be able to land anywhere on Eighty Mile Beach, which, according to their information, was "eighty miles of sand without a pebble." The Otter could refuel from the Halifax and proceed with its work while the Halifax returned to Darwin for a further load of petrol and oil. Whether this would work out as well in practice as in theory could only be ascertained by trial and error. As things turned out this did not arise.

The airfield chosen for a base in the first instance was Broome, a port on the coastal route developed by West Australian Airways. Not only was this the nearest available petrol supply to the area in which von Stalhein's party had first been sighted, but Biggles had a vague hope that he might pick up some information from the crews of the pearling luggers that made the town their home port.

Little news had come to hand, except the information for which Biggles had asked, since his first interview with the Air Commodore. The names given by von Stalhein's party had been checked, and it came as no surprise that they were unknown in Western Europe. The *See Taube* was not known in Hamburg, either.

Biggles had written a personal note to West, one of the control officers he had met on a previous occasion at Port Darwin, asking him to check up on the aircraft in which the "shipwrecked sailors" had left the town. From where had it come and to where had it gone? He, Biggles, would be along shortly to speak to him about it.

It had been learned that the spot where von Stalhein's boat had first been spotted was about twenty miles seaward from the southern end of the barren stretch of coast, south of Broome, known, and shown on the map, as Eighty Mile Beach, to which reference has already been made. As willie-willies, with their hundred and twenty miles an hour fury, come in broadly from a northerly direction, it was possible to form a rough idea of the most

14

probable direction of the island on which von Stalhein's ship had been cast away. A close study of the chart revealed no lack of islands, and Admiralty Sailing Directions gave descriptions of some of them. Mostly uninhabited, they varied in composition between stark coral reef and the shallow, blown-sand and sea-grass type, like the Lacepedes. Many bore the names of the early explorers or forgotten sea captains. As to the coast of the mainland, Ginger regarded with some concern the thousand miles of sand dunes backed for the most part by desert, with an occasional lonely mine or sheep station. There were towns, but they were few and far between. Ginger's eye followed them round—Derby, Broome, Hedland, Roebourne, Onslow. . . . He was relieved to note that most of them were served by air.

The Otter arrived first at Port Darwin. Biggles did not go ashore at once, for although his proposed excuse for being there was nothing more romantic than an equipment test in varying overseas conditions, he was afraid he might be thought a fit subject by a press photographer. Publicity was the last thing he wanted.

After dark, taking Ginger with him, he made his way to the airport buildings and reintroduced himself to West, and reminded him of his letter.

"What is it this time—another gold swindle?" inquired West, smiling.

"Nothing like it," answered Biggles. "Strictly between ourselves, we're looking for somebody, and we thought he might be in that party I told you about in my letter."

"Well, I'm sorry, but I haven't much news for you," was the disappointing reply. "The machine was a Qantas Airways Lockheed. Came up from Brisbane. I can give you the registration letters if that's any use to you. It went back to Brisbane, but Jimmy Alston, who was flying it, has an idea the people didn't stay there, because he saw them hanging about the airport some time after he'd booked in. He's been here since and I spoke to him about it. He hasn't been able to find out where they went after he unloaded them."

"Who paid for the flight? It must have been an expensive trip and it's unlikely the passengers had any money."

"Apparently a fellow named Smith. He paid in ready money. Nobody knew anything about him. Didn't matter much who he was, I reckon, as long as he had the cash."

"He didn't give any address?"

"If he did no one seems to have made a note of it. All Jimmy could get from the booking clerk was he spoke like a foreigner."

"Useful name, Smith," murmured Biggles. "And that's all you've been able to find out."

"That's the lot. Do you want me to ask Jimmy, if he comes up again, to try to find out more about this chap Smith?"

Biggles thought for a moment. "No thanks. It might do more harm than good. Of course, if he should see any of these people again, and that includes Smith, he might let you know and you could tell me. I expect to be around for a while. Is Alston on a regular run?"

"As a relief. He does most of the charter work. Must know his way round Australia better than anyone."

"I see. Well, many thanks. We'll get along."

"How long do you reckon to be here?"

"Not more than a day or two actually in Darwin, but I may be back later on. I'm waiting for a friend of mine to arrive. He's on the same job as I am, in a Halifax. We've arranged to meet here."

At this point of the conversation the door opened and a man in a captain's uniform came in. "I'm looking for Bigglesworth," he announced. "They tell me he's in the building."

"That's me," returned Biggles.

"I've got a message for you. I'm just in from Singapore. There's a friend of yours there, named Lacey, with an old Halifax. He told me to tell you he's hung up with a spot of engine trouble. Nothing serious; but it may be a day or two before he can get away. At the moment everyone's busy on a nasty crack-up on the airfield."

"Thanks," acknowledged Biggles. "Are you going back that way?"

"Day after tomorrow."

"Well, if he's still there when you get there you might tell him not to get in a flap. There's no hurry. If I'm not here when he gets here he'd better wait."

"Okay."

"Thanks a lot."

The pilot departed and Biggles turned to West. "If Lacey arrives and I'm not here you might tell him to concentrate on getting his machine a hundred per cent airworthy. This is no country to take chances."

West grinned. "Glad you've realised that. Are you thinking of pulling out right away now?"

"As I've nothing to do here I shall probably take a run down the coast to have a general look round. Oh, and that reminds me. Do you happen to know what became of the lifeboat in which those fellows came ashore?"

West shook his head. "It was never mentioned in my hearing. I gather it had been knocked about so it's unlikely that anyone would trouble to fetch it. I could probably find out for you. Len Seymour, one of our chaps was with the relief party. He'll have gone home now but I could ring him."

"I wish you would. It's only a detail, but every little helps."

West put through the call.

"It was left on the beach," he announced, as he hung up. "Len says they pulled it high and dry in case it was wanted, and left it there. There was nothing else they could do with it. It wasn't worth much, anyway."

"Thanks," acknowledged Biggles. "Well, we'll get along now. See you later, maybe."

Leaving the building they returned to the Otter.

"Pity about Algy," observed Ginger, on the way.

"If he's having trouble it's a good thing he's where he is, and not in the middle of nowhere."

"Are we going to a hotel for the night?"

"No. We'll sleep on board, then there will be no difficulty in making an early start."

"You're going straight on to have a look at the islands?"

"We might as well. I don't feel like sitting here doing nothing for perhaps a week. We'll have a wash, get a bite in the town and come back. It's under four miles so if we have to walk it won't do us any harm."

"Fair enough," agreed Ginger.

So they had a meal in Darwin, the little town which, practically unknown forty years ago, was 'put on the map' by aviation, and is now the focal point for planes arriving in, or leaving, Australia. A modest monument was erected to the memory of Ross Smith, the airman who, in his Vickers Vimy, first touched down on what was to become the first airport in Australia, with hangars, oil tanks,

17

workshops, and a beacon that can be seen for a hundred miles to guide machines making the night crossing of the Timor Sea.

Early to bed, morning saw Biggles and Ginger deflating their pneumatic mattresses while the stars still gleamed in the sky; and before the town was awake the Otter was droning down a south-westerly course on its six hundred mile run to the scene of its first investigation. To starboard lay the open sea, an indigo plain stretching to infinity in the light of the new-born day. To port, a few feathers of mist were drifting over the purple smudge that was Australia's lonely north-west coast—perhaps the most forsaken stretch of coast in the world.

Ginger knew that Biggles had no clear-cut plan of campaign. Islands, numbers of islands and atolls, any one of which might be the one they sought, were scattered far and wide. They were mostly small and uninhabited, but size was no indication. Biggles had admitted frankly that all they could do was take in turn each square that he had marked on the chart and fly low over any islands that fell within it. This, of course, meant a good deal of dead reckoning navigation for Ginger. The immediate objective was the spot where the rescue pilot had pinpointed the boat. Biggles had not bothered to look him up, feeling sure that he would not be able to tell them more than they already knew. The direction from which the boat had come could only be guesswork, and their guess was as good as his.

It was just after nine o'clock when Ginger announced that they were as near the pinpoint as he would be able to estimate it. The mainland, with its miles of untrodden sand, was a silvery streak on the horizon. The rest was open sea, without a ship, without an island, without a mark of any sort to break its sparkling surface.

Biggles turned the bows of the machine to the north and the search began.

To narrate in detail the hours that followed would be monotonous reiteration. Suffice it to say that several islands were examined without result. Biggles's method was to cruise low over the foreshore while Ginger watched for signs of wreckage. This was really easier than it may sound because most of the islands were low-lying, small and treeless, either coral atolls or banks of sand not more than eight or ten feet high at the highest point. These,

18

Biggles felt sure, would be overwhelmed in severe hurri-
canes. Once in a while there would be an island worthy of
the name, boasting an odd breadfruit tree or a few wind-
torn coconut palms.

There were several false alarms when what looked like
wreckage was sighted. On one occasion Biggles landed on
the tranquil surface of a lagoon; but the wreck turned out
to be barnacle and seaweed encrusted remains of an
unlucky lugger, lost, no doubt, in one of the notorious
willie-willies. They took the opportunity to have a rest,
and some food.

"These islets must be death-traps for ships in bad
weather," remarked Ginger.

"We should have taken into account the possibility of
sundry wreckage, apart from what we're looking for,"
replied Biggles. "More than once, I believe, the entire
pearling fleet has been wiped out. From November to
April, when a hurricane can blow up in an hour, pearling
must be an anxious business."

"I imagine you'll go to Broome for the night, and top
up the tanks?" supposed Ginger.

"I've been thinking about that," answered Biggles. "It
may not be necessary. I don't want to be seen there too
often. It struck me that we might carry on until near
sundown. Then, if we could find a safe anchorage we
could sit down for the night and finish this particular area
in the morning before heading for Broome. We're still
all right for juice."

Ginger agreed there was no sense in waffling a hundred
miles to the coast, only to come back in the morning, if it
could be avoided.

It was about four o'clock when Biggles pointed out a
lagoon that he thought should suit them. The time was
still on the early side, but as he said, they had had enough
flying for one day.

The lagoon was part of a typical coral atoll formation.
That is to say, the land that formed the island, at no point
more than twenty feet above sea level, was the shape of a
horseshoe. The open ends dwindled to mere points, and
then, continuing on as reefs of varying width, without
quite meeting, encompassed the flat sheet of water that
was the lagoon. This might have been half a mile in
diameter. The beach, the only beach, was a strip of sand
on the inside of the horseshoe. On the outer side, and,

indeed, all round the encircling reef, the ocean swell broke in showers of sparkling spray to the accompaniment of a dull continuous rumble. The only vegetation the island could produce was a little sparse scrub and a group of perhaps a dozen palms, their fronds torn and tattered, presumably by the recent willie-willie.

Ginger, who had seen atolls before, was not impressed. He was merely concerned with the safe anchorage it provided, and would provide while the weather remained calm. Ripples surged in through the opening in the reef, but for the most part the lagoon lay like a sheet of glass under a sky serenely blue.

As Biggles made a false run to check the surface for possible obstructions Ginger noticed several small white spots, scattered about the land, that he could not identify. Without being more than mildly curious he noted them in passing, recalling that he had seen similar spots on the last island they had surveyed. They hadn't landed, so he had had no opportunity of finding out what they were. The swish of the keel as it kissed the water, cutting a V-shaped ripple, put the objects out of his head; and for the next few minutes, after Biggles had taxied close inshore, they were busy making everything snug.

After that there was nothing more to do. Biggles took the Primus from its locker. "We'll have a cup of tea and then go ashore to stretch our legs," he suggested.

"Are you going to sleep on board?" asked Ginger.

"I don't think so. I'd rather sleep on the beach under the stars. We seem to have the place to ourselves and we're not likely to have visitors."

The only signs of life were, in fact, a few gulls that wheeled around the aircraft mewing their disapproval of it.

Under the water it was different, and although he had seen similar pictures before Ginger hung over the side gazing at that most fascinating of all spectacles, a coral garden. Through it, moving from one growth of coral to another, their shadows falling on the bottom, swam schools of brilliantly coloured fish. Most of these were small, but occasionally a big one would drift lazily into the picture, sending the little fellows darting for their lives.

At Biggles's call of tea-up he turned away reluctantly. "I'm having a swim when I've had my tea," he announced.

"That's a pleasant thought," agreed Biggles. "I'll keep watch for sharks while you're in, then you can keep watch for me. These seas are stiff with the brutes, but there shouldn't be anything of a dangerous size inside the lagoon. All the same, I'd rather not take a chance."

Tea finished, Ginger had his dip. Biggles followed, with Ginger standing in the centre-section, watching. But of the dreaded triangular fin he saw no sign.

By the time preparations had been made to spend the night ashore the sun was dropping like a ball of fire beyond the horizon.

CHAPTER III

AN UNCOMFORTABLE NIGHT

THERE are few things on earth more beautiful than an atoll on a still, moonlit night. The sunset dies. The colours fade. The palm fronds bow their heads and come silently to rest. Silver stains the eastern sky. The rim of the moon appears, and climbing, broadens, to cast an ethereal radiance across the ocean, the motionless lagoon, and the beach, which seems to float in space. A distant nightgull cries. A land-crab, emerging from its burrow, rattles his shelly legs on a pebble, interrupting for a moment an atmosphere that has taken on the solemnity of a cathedral.

It may have been this atmosphere that prevented Ginger from sleeping. Or it may have been the beauty or the strangeness of the scene. Sitting up on the warm sand he gazed at it, a little annoyed by this unusual wakefulness, particularly as Biggles was already fast asleep beside him. Certainly there was no thought of danger in his head.

In deep meditation he watched a broad ripple surge in through the opening in the reef. It travelled faster and came farther than most of them—the result, he supposed, of an extra big wave. Another followed. There seemed to be something odd about the ripple. Normally the ripples started at once to broaden, and losing their impetus died before they were half-way to the beach. But these particular ripples neither died nor broadened. They maintained a clearly defined arrow-head shape almost to the beach, as if made by an invisible boat. Yet a third of these unnatural ripples came in to set the reflected moon-beams flashing. Then a possible solution struck him. The disturbance could, he thought, be caused by turtles, coming ashore, as is their habit, to lay their eggs in the sand.

He watched for a time, but as there was no further development he lay back, with his head on his hands, to court the sleep without which the following day would find him dull and hot-eyed. But it was no use, and he realised that he had reached that state of wakefulness that made his brain ever more alert. There was only one thing to do, he decided, and that was to make a break of some sort. A short walk on the beach might do it.

Sitting up he glanced along the sand, and saw at once that one of the turtles had come ashore. Another was just emerging from the water. Then a frown creased his fore-head. These things weren't turtles. They were too big. They were the wrong shape. They looked more like large barrels, tapering at one end. With no other sensation than curiosity he watched, his proposed walk forgotten. He kept still for fear of alarming the creatures and sending them back into the sea before he could identify them.

A third beast now appeared, and it may have been the spider-like way it moved that gave him his first twinge of uneasiness. Whatever the things were, he decided, they were certainly not turtles. No turtle could make a sudden sideways dart. He didn't like the idea of waking Biggles, but when one of the beasts began moving furtively towards them he thought it time he did so. Putting a hand on Biggles's shoulder he gave him a slight shake.

"What is it?" asked Biggles instantly.

"I don't know; but I think you'd better have a look at these things," answered Ginger. "I don't like the look of 'em. They came in through the break in the reef—made a big ripple, too."

Biggles sat up. He looked. He looked for some time without speaking. But when, suddenly, one of the beasts raised itself up and flung out a long snake-like tentacle at something higher up the beach, he not only spoke, but moved fast. "By thunder!" he exclaimed tersely. "They're decapods. I don't know much about the ugly brutes but I believe they're dangerous. If they did decide to come for us we wouldn't have much chance. We'd better get into the machine."

Ginger wasted no time in splashing through the shallow water to the aircraft, which was afloat on about three feet of water ten or twelve yards from the beach. Turning to look back from the cabin door after Biggles had got in he saw one of the beasts moving swiftly, with a sinister gliding motion, towards the place where they had been. In the bright moonlight he could now see the tentacles plainly, two long ones, not less than twenty feet in length, held out in front, and a tangle of smaller ones. For the first time he realised too, the bulk of the creature's body. Feeling somewhat shaken he shut the door hurriedly. "What are you going to do?" he asked Biggles.

"Do? Nothing. They're not likely to come in here. I'm going to sleep." With that Biggles stretched himself out on the floor.

Ginger didn't feel much like going to sleep; but, naturally, any fears he may have had were allayed by Biggles's casual manner. From which it will be gathered that both of them were in blissful ignorance of the nature of the giant devil-fish, from which natives, who will attack an octopus or shark in its element with a knife, fly in terror.

Ginger had just fetched his mattress with the object of inflating it and trying to get some sleep when the aircraft gave a slight lurch. A flying boat rests very lightly on the water and it takes very little to make it move. A ripple or a gust of wind will do that. But, as Ginger knew well enough, a flying boat doesn't move on calm water of its own accord. He was pondering this strange occurrence when the machine took on a slight list, and instead of recovering remained in that position. This being beyond his understanding he dropped the mattress, and walking through the forward bulkhead door into the cockpit, looked for an explanation. It did not take him long to find it. With its great tentacles over the bows of the machine a giant squid was raising itself out of the water. Even as Ginger stared at a flat luminous eye the size of a tea plate the aircraft heeled over still further under the weight of the beast hanging on one side of it.

Biggles's voice came from the cabin. "What are you playing at? Why don't you keep still and get some sleep?"

Ginger swayed aft. In a thin, unnatural voice, he said:

"It wasn't me. It's one of those things. It's hanging on the side, as if it's trying to turn us over."

Biggles was on his feet in an instant, only to stagger as the machine took on a list of forty-five degrees. "If that thing gets hold of a wing it's liable to tear it off from the root," he said crisply. "Can you see the thing from the cockpit?"

"Yes."

"Load the rifle and bring it to me while I have a dekko." Biggles went forward. He looked, and, of course, saw what Ginger had seen, except that the beast was clear of the water, hanging across the bows. "The rifle—quick," he snapped.

Ginger moved fast. He loaded the rifle and handed it to Biggles. "Safety catch is on," he warned.

Very slowly Biggles adjusted his position and brought the rifle to his shoulder. Ginger, nearly sick with loathing and horror, could only watch, his heart behaving oddly. That one awful, cold, expressionless eye seemed to fascinate him, and at the same time take the strength out of his limbs.

The rifle crashed. Simultaneously the eye disappeared, as if it had been an electric lamp switched off. The aircraft righted itself with a jerk, nearly throwing Ginger off his feet. Then, to a great noise of splashing it began to rock, while every now and then something thudded against the hull, the keel, or some other part of the machine.

Clinging to the bulkhead door Ginger stared at Biggles aghast. "It'll smash us to pieces," he gasped.

"There's nothing more I can do," replied Biggles. "The thing's in the water. I don't know what it takes to kill these beasts, but as I aimed at the eye the bullet must have gone through its brain—if it's got one. This lashing may be its dying convulsions. I'm not going out to see, and perhaps be knocked overboard by one of those threshing tentacles."

The rocking became less violent, and going to a side window Ginger saw the reason. Twenty yards from the plane and moving away from it was an area of water being churned into foam. More than that, the side of the lagoon nearest to them appeared to have come to life, with ripples racing in all directions and moonlight dancing on the turbulence. Ginger could even see phosphorescent flashes under the water.

24

"I think other fish, knowing the brute's in its death throes, are rolling up for the feast," came Biggles's voice from the next window. "In the sea everything eats everything else."

"I hope the thing hasn't done any damage," muttered Ginger.

"I don't think so. We'll see presently. Fortunately it tried to come aboard by the bows. Had it tried to pull itself up on a wing something would certainly have been broken."

"It must have seen us come aboard, and followed."

"Possibly. Or it may have taken the aircraft for a new sort of bird, or fish."

"And to think we were bathing in that water this afternoon," Ginger shuddered.

"I doubt if the things were here then. I'd say they live in the deep water on the outer side of the reef, but come in at night to play about or look for food—land crabs, for instance."

"I shall think twice before I try sleeping on any more beaches in this part of the world," declared Ginger, warmly.

"It looks as if we shall have to swat up our natural history before we start on any more jaunts of this sort," averred Biggles. "Matter of fact I've heard of these big brutes but I've never seen one before. We must have struck a colony of 'em. I once had a spot of bother with a big octopus. That was bad enough. I've always been more concerned about sharks, no doubt because they are always around in tropic waters. But I think it's safe now for us to have a look round for any damage."

The churning had stopped. In fact, the lagoon had settled down, although tiny wavelets still ran up and down the beach. An examination, as far as this was possible in moonlight from the aircraft itself, revealed no sign of damage beyond some peeling of the paint on the bows, caused, it was assumed, by the great squid's suckers.

"Now, perhaps, we'll be allowed to get a little sleep," said Biggles irritably. "I don't think those things will trouble us any more tonight. I can see none on the beach, anyway. The danger might be sharks, brought in by the smell of blood—if those horrors have blood. Keep clear of the water."

"You needn't tell me to do that," returned Ginger, caustically.

Curiously, whereas before the disturbance he had been unable to sleep, he now dropped off, and when he awoke the sun was pouring an opalescent glaze, lovely to watch, on the ocean. Looking at the lagoon, once more clear and placid, he found it hard to believe that the events of the night were not an evil dream. "Are you thinking of going ashore again?" he asked Biggles, who was pumping up the Primus.

"There seems to be no point in it. Had there been anything to see we should have seen it."

"There's just one thing," returned Ginger. "As we came in I noticed some white spots that puzzled me. I saw some on another island, too. Thinking it over it struck me that they might be pieces of paper. I can't think of anything else they could be."

"You can soon settle that," answered Biggles. "Slip ashore while I'm making the tea. Five minutes should be enough."

"Okay," agreed Ginger.

It is, perhaps, unnecessary to say that he had a good look at the water before he stepped into it. However, seeing nothing he splashed quickly to the beach and made for the nearest of the objects that had aroused his curiosity. Approaching it, he saw that he had been right. He picked up a torn piece of newspaper, printed in German. The next piece was the same, crumpled and stained with salt water. Topping the ridge of atoll, which brought him facing a shingle beach on which the ocean rollers thundered, he saw there was more waste paper than he had supposed, for here it was less noticeable. First he picked up a typed list of what appeared to be names and addresses. It looked as if it had come adrift from a folio. His next find gave him a shock. All along the high water mark, mixed up with the usual medley of palm fronds, seaweed and shells, were Australian pound notes. He did not stop to collect them all, but picking up a few he hastened back to the aircraft. "I think we've struck something," he told Biggles briskly. "Take a look at these."

Biggles took the papers and studied them while Ginger poured himself a cup of tea and sat back to await his verdict.

"There's nothing to show what ship these came from," said Biggles after a while. "Other ships beside the *Taube* were lost in the hurricane, and these notes may have come from any of them."

"But an Australian pearling lugger wouldn't be likely to carry German newspapers."

"You're right there," agreed Biggles. "That, I own, is significant."

"What is that list?"

"Names and addresses—not in any particular town but several. Very odd. They may mean nothing to us, but if they do, they might mean a lot. The question is, how did these papers get here? There's no sign of a wreck, and these pieces of newspapers couldn't have been in the water very long or they'd have disintegrated."

"They could have been blown here by the wind."

"Yes. And on the face of a hundred mile an hour gale they might have travelled a long way. If we're right they must have come from the northerly quadrant."

"It was on an island north-west of here that I saw what I realise now must have been bits of paper. What about this money? Would a lugger be likely to pay its crew afloat? If not, why take a lot of money to sea? There's nowhere to spend it."

"I was thinking on the same lines," answered Biggles thoughtfully. "We'll go back to that island where you saw the paper. That should give us a direct line on the place this stuff started from. If we find nothing there of interest we'll carry on, following the line. It'll take us farther out to sea than I had reckoned to explore; but then, we've only von Stalhein's word that the party was on an island for three weeks. They could have been at sea longer than they pretended. Get the anchor up and we'll press on as far as we dare. We shall soon have to go to Broome for petrol."

In a few minutes the Otter was in the air, on the short run back to the last island it had surveyed without landing.

Reaching it, Biggles circled low, twice. "No sign of a wreck," he observed. "Surely there must be one somewhere. I don't think I'll waste time landing here. We'll push on over fresh ground and see if that produces anything."

Twenty minutes later, by which time he was beginning

27

to look more frequently at his petrol gauge, an island of some size crept up over the horizon. Ginger estimated it to be one of the seldom visited Mandeville Group. Even before they reached it they saw that the beach was strewn with wreckage.

"This looks more like it," remarked Biggles, with satisfaction in his voice. "Not much of a lagoon, but the water looks calm enough inside that reef."

Presently, after following the usual procedure, the Otter rocked gently to a standstill within a few yards of the debris-strewn beach on the sheltered side of the island. It was one of the largest they had visited, being nearly two miles long, about a quarter of a mile wide at the widest part, and better furnished with vegetation than most. There were several stands of coconut palms, although, like the others they had seen, they had suffered severely from the willie-willie.

Finding a bare patch of sand Biggles lowered his wheels and crawled up on to it, so that they could step out onto dry ground. "I'll tell you something right away," he said confidently. "This stuff represents more than one wreck." He pointed. "That broken mast with a bit of sail still wrapped round it was never part of a deep sea ship. The mast, and those splintered spars, could have been on a lugger. That reef may have been the one von Stalhein's vessel struck, and broke up, in which case I imagine most of it would go down in the deep water on the far side. I suppose it wouldn't be remarkable if a lugger, caught in the same storm, fell foul of the same island. But let's get busy. We've plenty to do."

The search began; not for any particular object, but for anything that might indicate the purpose of von Stalhein and his party in Australian waters. At least, Biggles affirmed, they would almost certainly come upon something carrying the names of the vessels that had been cast away.

In this, however, they were to be disappointed.

CHAPTER IV

ISLAND WITHOUT A NAME

THE first sign of tragedy lay on the beach. It was a skeleton. A few shreds of material still clung to it, but gave no clue to the nationality of the dead seaman. Ginger questioned whether it could be a casualty of the last willie-willie, or of a previous one.

"I'd say the last," replied Biggles. "I imagine the gulls would soon make short work of a body, human or otherwise. Besides, when the storm was actually on, wind and waves would have broken up a skeleton had it been lying here then."

They found more skeletons. Aside from these grisly souvenirs of disaster the search went on for an hour or more without producing anything of real interest. There were one or two magazines and scraps of paper but they had been reduced to pulp. Ginger found the stiff covers of a document file, but any papers that it had contained were missing. But a single word, stamped with a rubber stamp on the front, was significant. It was *Vertraulich*.

"Confidential," translated Biggles. "Evidently a confidential file. Pity the contents have gone. Anyway, it tells us that a German ship, carrying secret papers, was wrecked here, or near here."

"That list of addresses I picked up could have come from that file," said Ginger. "The size is the same."

"Could be," conceded Biggles. "A file is only used normally to hold several papers, so I suspect that sheet of addresses wasn't the only one. I noticed that of the addresses shown there wasn't one in Sydney or Melbourne. It seems hardly likely that places of that size would be omitted from a complete list, from which I conclude they occurred on pages other than the one we have. But we'll talk about that later. I think we can take it that von Stalhein's story of being shipwrecked was substantially true. But we assumed that already. His party wouldn't have put to sea in an open boat as a matter of choice. It's queer there's nothing with a name on. I have a feeling that anything of that nature was deliberately destroyed. A wooden object, or a cork lifebelt, could easily have been burnt. We've seen the marks of at least one good bonfire. What's this thing?"

A handle stuck up at an angle from the sand. He took hold of it and pulled. The object to which it was attached emerged. He shook the sand from it, and after a brief inspection the face that he turned to Ginger wore a curious smile. "Now we're getting somewhere," he said softly. "No lugger would be likely to carry that."

"A Geiger Counter,"* breathed Ginger.

"It looks as if von Stalhein *may* have had some scientists with him; but that isn't to say they were interested in fish. At first sight it looks as if we may have discovered the purpose of that ship in these waters."

"You mean, to make tests around the Montebello Islands, where we exploded atomic bombs."

"That could be one of the reasons."

"How far are we from the islands?"

"For a rough guess four hundred miles."

"That sounds a long way."

"The Americans issued a warning to shipping within four hundred and fifty miles of the Marshall Group, where they exploded their bombs. Von Stalhein and his friends may have been going nearer to the Montebello Group for all we know. But let's not jump to conclusions and say the mystery of the spy ship in these waters has been solved. The Geiger Counter is also used for other purposes; for locating uranium deposits in the ground, for instance. Anyway, it's an interesting discovery. We'll take the thing with us when we go." Biggles raised his head and sniffed. "Can you smell anything?"

"I've noticed a pretty offensive stink once or twice, if that's what you mean."

"That's exactly what I mean. It's corruption of some sort. It can only come on the breeze so whatever it is should be in this direction. Let's see."

A walk of some distance, with the smell becoming stronger, took them inland to an area of scrub that had not been explored, for the search, naturally, had been confined to the foreshore. Biggles approached cautiously —stopped—and then, after taking a few quick paces

* A device for the detection and counting of fast electrical particles, as from radio-active materials.

forward, stopped again, his handkerchief to his nose, bending over something. "You'd better stay where you are," he told Ginger. "This isn't pretty."

Ginger waited. Minutes passed. Then Biggles, looking a little pale, rejoined him. "Things outside my calculations have happened here," he announced grimly.

"What was it?"

"A man. Or what's left of one. I don't think he could have been dead more than a week or ten days."

"A white man?"

"No. An oriental. I'd say Japanese, or a mixed breed. He must have been on the lugger. I seem to remember that most of the pearling fleet is manned by Japanese types, Malays, or Asiatics of some sort. I fancy he was the skipper or he wouldn't have had this on him." Biggles opened a hand to disclose a small tobacco tin. He lifted the lid.

Ginger's eyes went round. "Pearls!"

"Naturally, that would be the one thing he'd try to save when he knew his ship was done for."

"But how—why did he stay, when——"

"Just a minute and I'll answer your questions, although, by thunder, they leave more to be answered. He was shot—at least twice. He was hit in the stomach and in the leg. His clothes are stiff with dried blood. And he didn't commit suicide, although he had this gun lying near his hand." Biggles took the revolver from his pocket, and "broke" it to show that four shots had been fired. A man determined to kill himself doesn't shoot himself in the leg."

"He was murdered."

"He was certainly shot by somebody and that looks mighty like murder. As I see it, hard hit, the poor devil clawed his way into these bushes to escape from whoever was after him."

"Mutiny."

Biggles shrugged. "Could have been; but was this the time and place for a mutiny? Think. The lugger had been battered to death by a hurricane. One man, probably several, managed to get ashore. And here they were, cast away, with little hope, as far as one can see, of ever getting off. I repeat, was that the moment for the survivors to start shooting each other?"

"One would hardly think so."

"Then how did this shooting come about?"

"There may have been a shortage of food. Some members of the crew shot the others in order to make it go round."

"Where are they? There's nobody here, alive, or we'd have seen them."

"They might have got away in a small boat."

"Would they, do you think, have gone without these?" Biggles held out the pearl tin. "They must have known about them. Would they have gone knowing that somewhere on the island there was a small fortune to be picked up?"

"Shouldn't think so."

"On the face of it these pearls might well have been the motive for murder. Yet they were left behind. That doesn't make sense. No, that isn't the answer. If it comes to that, if one man was shot it's possible that others were shot—those on the beach, who we assumed to have been drowned. Were they shot? Let's see."

Without speaking they returned to the beach, and the nearest skeleton.

Biggles dropped on his knees beside it and began lifting the bones carefully and putting them on one side. A ring fell from a bony finger. A signet ring. He picked it up and looked at the device on it. "Oriental," he said. "Apparently another member of the lugger's crew. Ah! Here we are. This is what I was looking for." He held out, in the palm of his hand, a bullet, slightly flattened. "Looks mighty like a Luger to me. I'll keep this. It may tell a tale one day." Putting it in his pocket he got to his feet.

"There seems to have been a battle here," said Ginger, looking shaken by this unexpected development.

"We could probably find more bullets if we went through the other skeletons, but I shan't bother. What we have seen tells us enough about that aspect of what happened here."

"But what could the fighting have been about if it wasn't pearls?"

"You haven't forgotten that another ship went ashore here?"

"No. But as all these survivors would be in the same boat why should they set about each other?"

"That's just it. They weren't in the same boat. There wasn't room for all of them."

32

Ginger stared.

"If you were cast away here pearls wouldn't be much use to you. Only one thing could help you."

"A boat."

"That's how it looks to me. There was one boat—and more people than could get into it. Von Stalhein's party got possession of it. Whether it was their boat, or a boat belonging to the lugger, I don't know. But we'll soon find out. That boat should still be on Eighty Mile Beach, and it should have a name on it. I say it *should* have. I don't say it has. But if it hasn't we shall know why. Let's go and look. We should have enough fuel to take in the Beach on our way to Broome for a fill-up. Come on. We know where this island is should we decide to return to it. It doesn't appear to have a name."

As they walked briskly to the Otter, Ginger asked: "What are you going to do with the pearls?"

"Find the rightful owner and hand them over. We shall have to report what we've seen today even if we don't do it right away. It isn't just a matter of the pearls, although the large pink one in particular should be worth a lot of money. It's a matter of suspected murder, and failure to report a thing like that might subject us to criticism, if nothing worse. For the moment I'll keep an open mind about it."

The Otter was soon on its way to the mainland, on a course calculated to bring it to Eighty Mile Beach below the estimated position of the abandoned lifeboat. The idea then was to fly along the beach, and after looking at the boat carry on to Broome.

On striking the vast curve of deserted sand, stretching away on either side as far as the eye could see, Biggles made a left hand turn, took the machine to something under a hundred feet and settled down to as slow a cruising speed as was compatible with safe flying. They expected no difficulty in spotting the boat on the flat, unbroken, wind-borne sand. Nor did they, although the sand had silted against it on one side and overflowed into the boat itself. On such a boundless airfield a landing presented no difficulty. Biggles dropped his wheels, put the machine down with hardly a tremor and taxied right up to the little craft that would go to sea no more. In a couple of minutes they were both standing by it.

"No name on the bows or the stern," muttered Biggles.

33

"Just what I expected." On the bows it had been scraped out. On the stern a piece of new timber had been let in. "Well, that tells us plenty. If the boat had belonged to the *See Taube* there would have been no need to remove the name—always supposing that *See Taube* was really the name of von Stalhein's ship. My guess, and I think it's a pretty safe one, is that this boat belonged to the lost lugger. It was, I fancy, the motive for the murders. Try to carry a description of the boat in your head in case I forget anything. In Broome we should be able to settle any argument. What happened on that island we may never know, but there should be no difficulty in identifying the lost lugger by my description of the dead man. Broome isn't all that big. Let's get along."

Biggles said little on the short flight to the airfield. Clearly preoccupied with the problems that had arisen, Ginger did not interrupt his thoughts. However, when the white-roofed township appeared ahead Biggles said: "To save time I'm going to leave you to attend to the refuelling. When you're through, take the small-kit to the Continental Hotel. We'll sleep there tonight. I've some enquiries to make, and I've decided that the safest— and the quickest— way, would be to go to the police. They'll keep quiet if I ask them. Otherwise we might be fiddling about here for days."

"Okay," agreed Ginger.

CHAPTER V

A WORD WITH SERGEANT GILSON

LEAVING Ginger at the airport, Biggles made his way through white-roofed bungalows, palms and poinciana trees, to the Port of Pearls that nestles beside the blue waters of Dampier Creek. With shell-grit crunching under his shoes he sought the police station, where he found Sergeant William Gilson in charge, and introduced himself by putting his credentials on his desk.

The Sergeant, tall, clear-eyed and sun-tanned, a fine figure of a man in his uniform, read the documents. Getting up he closed the door, resumed his seat, and looked enquiringly at Biggles, who was replacing his papers in his breast pocket. "Take a seat," he invited. "It must be something important to bring you all this way," he observed shrewdly.

"It's important to me, it's important to you, and it may be more important still for Australia," answered Biggles. "In fact, it's so important that I thought hard before coming even to you. But you may be able to help me. In all seriousness I warn you that if word of this conversation leaks out, with my name attached to it, you may do your country an immense amount of harm."

"I can keep my trap shut," promised Gilson, a trifle curtly.

"Then first I shall have to tell you what brings me to Australia. You will recall, following the recent willie-willie, seven survivors of a wrecked ship came ashore on Eighty Mile Beach?"

"I remember it."

"One of those men is, and has been for many years, the most notorious enemy agent in Europe. He hates us, which means he hates you. He is now in Australia."

"What does he want here?"

"That's what I'd like to know, and what I'm here to find out. As he may be anywhere in Australia you'll appreciate I have a job on my hands."

"You certainly have."

"I've been having a look round, and it's what I've found that has brought me to you. In answering my questions you may learn a thing or two yourself. How many ships were lost from your fleet here in the last willie-willie?"

"Three. We know where one went ashore so call it two."

"Was the skipper of one of them a man, probably a Japanese, stockily built, about five foot four in height, with a gold-filled tooth in the upper jaw?"

"He was. That'd be Toto Wada—an Australian-Jap. Nice quiet chap. Used to be a diver till he bought his own lugger."

"Just to make sure. Did you ever see the thing in which he carried his pearls?"

"Often. It was a two ounce tobacco tin."

"Like this?" Biggles put the box on the table.

"That's the one."

35

"Then you'd better take charge of it for his next of kin."

"That's his wife. Lives in Sheba Lane."

The sergeant's eyes opened wide when Biggles held the tin so that the contents could be seen. "How did you get that? Where's Toto?"

"He won't be coming back. He's dead. His lugger went ashore on an island and broke up. He got ashore, and so did at least one of the crew. This ring may help you to identify him. Both men were subsequently shot. I found the bodies."

"Shot! How the—who the——"

"A German ship went ashore on the same island. There were Germans in the party that landed on Eighty Mile Beach. You'll see what I'm getting at."

Gilson's brow was black. "Yes. I see," he said slowly.

"That brings us to the boat," resumed Biggles. "I've just looked at the boat that brought these foreigners ashore. It's a brown-varnished clinker-built job about twenty-two feet long and four foot beam. Rather high in front, plenty of freeboard——"

"You needn't say any more," interposed the sergeant. "I know that boat. It belonged to Toto."

"That's how I worked it out; and that's why I decided I'd have to tell you about it. Frankly, the fate of this unfortunate pearler is no concern of mine, because it isn't going to help me much in my search for the man I'm looking for. I'd rather you said nothing about it for the moment; but you might keep your ears open, and if you hear any local talk about a strange ship being seen off the coast between, say Wyndham and Perth, let me know. Incidentally, you'd better have these. They may be needed as evidence one day." Biggles pushed two bullets and a ring across the desk. "These are two of the shots that did the murders. The ring was on what was left of the finger of one of the crew."

"And you're asking me to do nothing about this?" Gilson looked doubtful.

"Yes. I'm asking you because there's more at stake than the shooting of one or two pearlers. If you start making inquiries on your own account you may upset my applecart. I know the man I'm looking for. Leave him to me—unless, of course, you hear that I've made a boob and got myself shot." Biggles smiled. "Should that happen, and it might, compare the bullet with those on your desk."

"All right," agreed Gilson reluctantly. "If that's how you want it. We'll leave it like that for the time being. You let me know when I can go ahead but don't leave it too long."

"Not longer than is absolutely necessary," promised Biggles. "Now I wonder if by any chance you can help me with this." He took from his pocket the list of names and addresses Ginger had picked up. "Do any of those names mean anything to you? I mean, have any of them, to your knowledge, a police record?"

Gilson studied the list. "No," he stated, when he came to the end. "But don't take my word for it. I only deal with local cases, although local in this part of the world covers a pretty wide area—most of it desert, of course. There are two places here I've never even heard of. This Tarracooma Creek is one."

"It says Tarracooma Creek, Western Australia. We're in West Australia now."

"All the same I've never heard of it. Must be a small place. But then, Western Australia is a lot of ground and there are probably a lot of places I've never heard of, particularly farther south. I'll ask Old Joe Hopkins when he comes in. He's overdue, so he shouldn't be long. He may know. He used to ride the Fence.* He's a digger— what you'd call a prospector—now, and knows the country better than most people."

"What about the name of the man—Roth? Does that mean nothing to you?"

"Not a thing."

"What about the other place. Daly Flats, Northern Territory?"

"I've never heard of that either. Nor do I know the man's name—Boller. All I know of the Territory is what I read in the papers. I'll tell you what I'll do if you like. I see one of these addresses is in Perth. Chap named Adamsen. I could put a call through to our office there and ask them if they know anything about him."

"That might save me a trip there."

* The rabbit-proof fence which crosses the continental deserts from north to south. It is patrolled by riders who repair any damage done by the larger wild creatures—kangaroos, wallabies, emus, and the like.

"Come through. I'll get the missus to make you a cup of tea while you're waiting."

"Thanks. That would be very welcome."

Biggles was shown into the sitting-room where he chatted with the policeman's family for nearly half an hour.

"Not much to tell you," reported Gilson, when he came back. "There are no convictions against Adamsen, but they know him for an agitator, trouble-maker, and so on. He's an electrician by trade. Politically he's a red-hot Communist of the loud-mouthed type."

"Ah," breathed Biggles. "That's very interesting. It fits in with what I know."

"But look here," went on Gilson. "Thinking things over while I was waiting for that call, you seem to have put me on a bit of a spot."

"How so?"

"This business of Wada and his lugger. No offence meant, but I've never seen you before and I've only your word for it. That's okay with me, but a court would want evidence of identification. You didn't know Wada by sight, so your word that he was dead could be disputed."

"Yes. I see your point," agreed Biggles pensively.

"What's the name of this island?"

"If it has one I don't know it. It's one of a scattered group, all on the small side, north-east of the Rowley Shoals."

"How far do you reckon it to be from here?"

"Two hundred miles, more or less."

"That's a long way."

"How do you mean?"

"Well, let's be frank about it. I ought to go and look at the body—maybe bring it back here for burial. I knew the man well. There could then be no argument about his death. You've got to produce a body before you can charge anyone with murder."

"True enough. Very well. Why not go and verify my story?"

"How am I going to do that without bringing you into it? To start with I should have to apply for transport, and as I couldn't do that without giving reasons it would mean letting your cat out of the bag."

"That is a bit awkward," agreed Biggles. "Suppose I

flew you out to the island. Would that solve your problems?"

Gilson thought for a moment. "Yes, that'd do it. I suppose we could do the job in a day?"

"Easily. If that's agreed, the sooner we go the better. What about tomorrow?"

"Suits me."

"Say, six o'clock tomorrow morning at the airfield."

"Okay, I'll be there."

"Good. Then I'll get along. Thanks for being so helpful."

They shook hands and Biggles departed, thinking hard.

He found Ginger waiting in the hotel lounge. "Did you get the tanks topped up?" he asked, dropping into the next chair.

"No trouble at all," Ginger assured him. "What's your news?"

"In a nutshell: the lugger that went ashore on the island came from here. The body I found was the owner, a Japanese named Wada. The boat that brought von Stalhein and his party ashore belonged to the lugger. That all ties up with what we surmised. But what has set me thinking is this. Gilson, the police-sergeant, was helpful enough to check up on one of the names and addresses on that list you picked up. Adamsen, of Perth. It seems he's a trouble-making agitator. The question is, how does he fit into the von Stalhein set-up?"

"If he isn't actually on the Iron Curtain pay-roll now he may have been listed as a prospective recruit."

"If that's the case we must assume that the same applies to others on the list. Who compiled that list? There's only one answer. An agent already planted here. With what object?"

"To complete a network of spies against the time they'll be needed."

"I don't like the sound of that. If you're right, then this is a more dangerous scheme than I had supposed. The trouble is, while these people remain passive they're within the law and there's nothing we can do about it beyond providing the Dominion with the gen so that on the outbreak of a war they could chuck a net over the whole bunch."

"If the von Stalhein gang intends to contact Adamsen and the others, by watching we might grab them—or

39

tip off the police. We've got a case against them—for murder."

"We shall have, I hope, by this time tomorrow. We're flying Gilson out to have a look at things. He knew Wada and will be able to provide evidence of identification. He's meeting us at the airfield at six."

"While we're there we might have another look round for some more pages from that file."

"That's a good idea; but we can't spend too long there. Gilson wants to get back and I shall have to find out what Algy's doing. Let's see about something to eat."

CHAPTER VI

FORESTALLED

THE following morning the Otter left Broome on the hour, and just before seven the Island without a Name crept up over the horizon.

Bill Gilson—for in the easy going Australian manner they were now calling each other by their Christian names—who had evidently done some serious thinking about the affair, was now taking more than a passing interest in it, and posed questions for which so far there was no answer. Naturally, he inclined towards the official police angle. Biggles revealed what he knew, and what he surmised.

"The snag where you're concerned is this," Biggles told him. "Putting aside for the moment the question of murder, until you have proof that this gang is working against the interests of Australia there's no point in taking them to court."

"Murder is plenty of reason," muttered Bill, grimly.

"All right. Hang the lot—and then where are you? The purpose for which these people came here would be carried on by a fresh gang unknown to us. I believe now that I started off on the wrong foot. The first things that came into my head when I knew von Stalhein was here was the new rocket range, the atom bomb experimental sites and the uranium workings. They, of course, are

40

bound to come into the picture; but I now suspect that the plot goes deeper than that. What I see now is a wide-spread organisation that will not only keep the Iron Curtain countries informed of technical developments here, but might, by fomenting strikes and the like, upset your entire economy."

"You mean, through Communist propaganda?"

"Call it that if you like; but Communism, in the place where it started, is now a handy political name for a military-minded clique that suffers from the old ambition of world domination. The trouble is, few of the people who get drawn into the thing realise that they're lining up with a potential enemy, or that a cold war is just as deadly as a hot one. They're never likely to get anything out of it, anyway. Of course, there are some who go Red in order to work off a grudge. Von Stalhein is a case in point. With him it's personal. He hates us because Hitler lost the war. When he was a Nazi he hated Communism, and I'd wager he still does. But he'll work for the Iron Curtain brigade because it offers him a way to have another crack at us. For that he has sacrificed his sense of humour, and any pleasure he might have got out of life."

"I gather he's pretty tough."

"Tough?" Biggles smiled wanly. "He's so tough that if you hit him in the face with a stone the stone would go to pieces."

With the island within gliding distance Biggles cut his engines and idled on. But as the calm water within the reef came into view he stiffened suddenly, staring through the windscreen. "Do you see what I see?" he asked sharply.

"A ship," said Ginger tersely.

"Lugger," observed Bill, laconically, from behind Biggles's shoulder.

"What do you make of that?" queried Biggles, gliding on.

"Your guess is as good as mine. One lugger is much like another. Could be a pearler, put in for some reason or other. All I can say is it isn't one of the Broome fleet."

"I can see people on the island . . . walking about . . . blacks as well as whites," observed Ginger.

"Most luggers carry coloured crews," said Bill.

"They haven't heard us or they'd be looking up," said Ginger.

"The rollers on the reef, and on the windward side, would prevent them from hearing anything," asserted Bill. "I'd say it's just an odd chance that brought the lugger here."

"We shall soon know," murmured Biggles, sideslipping off a little height to glide straight in. "I shan't run her up on the beach—she might as well stay afloat for the short time we shall be here."

No more was said. The machine glided on, silently, the steady thunder of the breakers drowning any slight noise it might have made. There was no one on the deck of the lugger. The men ashore did not look up. From water level they were concealed by the scrub and the contours of the ground, so it seemed that the Otter made its landing unobserved. But as soon as Biggles touched his throttle to take the aircraft right on to the lugger a man appeared on deck, hurriedly, and, as it seemed to Ginger, in a state of startled agitation—although, in the circumstances, the reason for this might have been natural, and innocent enough. He was a big man, black-bearded, and roughly dressed.

Bill read aloud the name on the vessel's stern, "*Matilda. Darwin.*"

Biggles took the Otter into shallow water near the lugger. Ginger went forward and dropped the anchor. Bill, who was of course in uniform, hailed the ship. "Hello, there! Are you all right?"

"Yes," came the answer.

"What are you doing?"

"Picking up a few fresh nuts."

"You're a long way from home."

"With the water picked clean it's time someone looked for new ground."

Bill turned to Biggles. "I wouldn't call the man a liar but neither would I bet he's telling the truth," he said suspiciously. "Still, his business isn't likely to be ours so let's get on with the job."

"Just a minute," returned Biggles. "There should be two skeletons lying on that beach within forty yards of us. They've gone. Bones don't walk."

"The *Matilda's* crew may have buried 'em."

"Could be," agreed Biggles dubiously. "Ginger, there's no need for you to come ashore. Stay here and watch the machine."

"All right." Ginger, looking at Biggles's face, knew that he was puzzled by finding the *Matilda* there, and was not entirely satisfied by the explanation given by the man who was presumably the skipper. As Biggles and Bill stepped out and waded ashore he sat in the cockpit to watch events. Blackbeard, too, he noticed, was also watching, leaning on the rail, smoking a pipe; but there was something about his attitude that gave Ginger a feeling that this nonchalance was affected rather than genuine. What, he wondered, were the men ashore doing?

He wondered still more when, a few minutes later, two white and eight coloured men came into sight from the direction of the thick scrub. Two blacks carried implements that were either spades or shovels. The party, still some distance away, seemed to be in a great hurry, the blacks being urged into a run by a brown-skinned man whose better style of dress suggested that he was in charge—possibly the mate of the lugger.

Ginger realised with a twinge of uneasiness that Biggles and Bill had not seen this procession, for they had already disappeared over the low ridge that formed the backbone of the island when it appeared. The thing struck him as being deliberate rather than accidental—as if the party had been watching, waiting for Bill and Biggles to get out of sight before showing themselves.

Ginger's feeling of uneasiness mounted. Although he told himself that there was no reason for this he became increasingly aware that he was alone, with the others out of earshot. The booming of the breakers on the reef would smother any call for help. It was, therefore, with some anxiety that he watched the shore party hurry on towards their dinghy that had been pulled up on the beach.

He glanced at the lugger, twenty yards away, and saw that blackbeard was watching him surreptitiously. Did that mean anything—or nothing? There was no answer to that, but he perceived with a sudden wave of apprehension what their position would be if anything happened to the aircraft—a thought that was no doubt prompted by the close proximity of the two craft. He wished fervently that the machine had been moored farther away.

Again turning his attention to the shore party he saw that it had now reached the dinghy. Under the directions of the brown man, a big, fierce-looking Malay, it was hauled on to the water. Some of the blacks started to swim to the lugger. The white men moved forward to board the dinghy. One of them, Ginger noticed, walked with a slight limp. Suddenly there was something familiar about his figure. Ginger stared incredulously, telling himself that it was impossible, even though he knew his eyes were not deceiving him. The man was Erich von Stalhein.

For an instant Ginger remained rigid from shock, for the possibility of such an encounter was beyond the limits of his imagination. Recognition, he knew, was largely a matter of time and place. He had not associated von Stalhein with a pearling lugger, or, for that matter, with a desert island; and that, he could only conclude, was why he hadn't recognised him earlier.

By this time the peril of his position had overcome the first stunning shock, and he was moving. What Blackbeard would do when his crew was aboard he didn't know; nor did he waste time guessing. Only one thing mattered, and that was to get the machine well clear of the lugger.

Going forward, trying to behave as if his actions were of no real importance, he hauled in the anchor and returned to the cockpit. Out of the corner of his eye he could see Blackbeard beckoning the dinghy, although it was now nearly alongside. The Malay caught a rope, swarmed up it, and joined Blackbeard in a swift conversation.

Ginger waited for no more. The Otter, fanned by a slight breeze, was already drifting, but nothing like fast enough; for the lugger's anchor was now coming up, and its propeller churning the water into foam set the machine rocking.

The Otter's engines came to life. Even so, Ginger saw that it was going to be touch and go, for the lugger, ostensibly turning, was backing into his tail unit. Instinctively he shouted a warning, although he knew he was wasting his breath. The trouble was, he, too, had to turn to get clear, or run aground.

With teeth clenched, expecting every instant to hear the crash of a collision that would crumple his tail like tissue paper, he brought her bows round to open water. Even when the machine bounded forward under full throttle he was still not sure that he had escaped damage, for the roar of her engines drowned all other sounds and the hull was rocking in the turbulence caused by the lugger's screw.

It was for this reason, because he was not certain that the machine was airworthy, that he did not actually leave the water. As soon as he was sure that he was clear he throttled back and merely skimmed on to the far side of the area of calm water, where he jumped up to ascertain if the aircraft had suffered damage. To his great relief all appeared to be well, so turning to open water, ready to take off should it become necessary, he looked to see what the lugger was doing. His nerves relaxed when he saw that it was heading at full speed for the open sea.

Biggles and Bill were running down the beach.

After waiting for a minute to recover his composure, for he had been badly shaken, he turned again and cruised slowly towards them.

"What on earth are you doing?" was Biggles's greeting.

"You might well ask," answered Ginger grimly. He jerked a thumb at the retreating lugger. "Those devils tried to ram me. Nearly got me, too. I recognised him just in time."

"Recognised who?"

"Von Stalhein."

It was Biggles's turn to stare. "You mean—he's in that ship?"

"He was on the island at the same time as you—with as pretty a gang of toughs as you ever saw. From the way they ran back to the lugger I have an idea they spotted you. Or if von Stalhein didn't actually recognise you he must have taken a dislike to Bill's uniform."

"Then what happened?"

"I had a feeling they might try something so I got cracking on a quick move. It took me a minute to get the hook up and by that time the lugger was backing into me. I must have got clear by a whisker. It may have looked like an accident, but it wasn't. They knew what they were doing all right. Had they sunk me, or stove my tail in, we should have been three Robinson Crusoes without even a parrot."

Biggles looked at Bill. "So now we know," he said simply.

"What do you know?" asked Ginger.

"Why Wada's body has disappeared. That goes for the skeleton's, too. No bodies, no murder. Trust von

45

Stalhein to think of that. He came back here to clean up—perhaps look for any papers that were left about. Those lists of names, for instance. It might take him some time to get a duplicate set from where they originated."

"I take it you didn't find any."

"We did not. We didn't get much time to look. Your engines starting up brought us back in a hurry."

"They've buried Wada's body," said Ginger. "At any rate, I assume that they've buried something because two of the crew were carrying shovels."

"Who was with von Stalhein?" asked Biggles.

"There was only one other white man in the party. I can't say that I recognised him but I've an idea he was one of the bunch in the photograph. A hair-cut and a shave would alter his appearance."

Bill stepped into the conversation. "I could still get this guy von Stalhein. I realise that there's nothing we can do about the lugger at the moment; but we know her name and we shall be home first. What about meeting him when he steps ashore?"

Biggles smiled wanly. "You don't know von Stalhein. Even if he didn't recognise me he must know that the arrival of an aircraft and a policeman at an out-of-the-way island like this was no mere fluke. Note how he took the precaution of coming back here to clean the place up. No doubt by this time his brain is busy working out what we're likely to do next."

"I'll get him," declared Bill doggedly.

"All right. And what are you going to do with him when you've got him? Even if you dug up the whole island and found Wada's body you still wouldn't be able to prove that von Stalhein did the shooting. In fact, knowing how he works, I'd risk a small bet that he didn't pull a trigger. He's a wily bird, and he'd leave that to someone else. Suppose you did grab him, and examined his gun—and found it clean? Or a different calibre from those bullets I gave you? He'd laugh at you, and you'd have exposed your hand for nothing."

"Are you suggesting that we let him walk away scot free?"

"Certainly not. I'm merely trying to point out that we may do more harm than good by going off at half cock, whichever way we look at it, yours or mine."

"What do you mean?"

"You, naturally, are concerned about a murder that has been committed. To me that's only a side issue. I've got to find out what von Stalhein and his gang are doing in Australia, and stop them at it, before they can do worse mischief than murder. To me the important thing about our trip here is the name of that lugger. The owner, or the skipper—probably the same—is in the racket, and that should lead us somewhere. My next step will be to check up on the *Matilda* at Darwin. I own freely that it didn't occur to me that von Stalhein might come back here. It might have been to cover up his tracks, or there may have been other reasons. He may have needed money. We found some notes. He may have hoped to find some instruments that were lost. We found a Geiger Counter. But let's not waste time guessing. The fact remains, he came back, and he has presumably destroyed all evidence of what happened here. I suggest that as we're here we might as well have a look round in case anything was overlooked. Then I'll take you home and push on to Darwin."

"Okay," agreed Bill.

They went ashore, but as Biggles had feared, a search of some three hours yielded not a single item of interest. Bill tramped the island from end to end looking for signs of digging, still hoping to find the body of the murdered man; but in the end, to his annoyance, he had to give it up.

"I'm afraid von Stalhein made a clean sweep while he was here," remarked Biggles, as they returned to the aircraft and snatched a makeshift lunch.

"There's still one piece of evidence he may find hard to explain," growled Bill.

"What's that?"

"The boat. You say it's still on Eighty Mile Beach. How's he going to account for coming ashore in a boat belonging to Wada's lugger? Several witnesses could describe the boat, and that should be good enough."

"Yes," agreed Biggles. "That would certainly take a lot of explaining."

"I ought to have a look at it. Just where is it?"

"Roughly about sixty miles south of Roebuck Bay. If you like, to save you a journey, we could take it in on the run home. It wouldn't be far out of our way."

"That'd suit me fine," declared Bill. "Save a lot of time and trouble."

"All right. If we've finished we might as well press on."

Biggles took the same course as before to the mainland, and again, flying low, cruised up the Beach. But even while he was still short of the position of the boat he was staring hard at it.

"Something's happened down there," observed Ginger.

"So I see," returned Biggles, shortly.

"Looks as if someone's had a fire."

Answered Biggles, in a curious voice: "It also looks as if another plane has landed since we were here. I can see two sets of wheel tracks and only one of them is mine—the wide, heavy one. There are more footmarks, too, than we made."

"The boat isn't there!"

"The black spot marks the place where it was. Someone's had a bonfire, and he didn't light it to keep himself warm. Recently, too. It's still smouldering."

"What's that you're saying?" put in Bill, from behind.

"The boat's gone. Someone has beaten us to it," replied Biggles.

For a moment Bill was shocked to silence. Then he swore softly.

"Now you see the sort of people we're up against," Biggles told him, as he glided in to land. "They leave nothing to chance."

He put the machine down and taxied up to the still smouldering embers—all that remained of the boat. They got out and looked at it.

"The job was done this morning," muttered Bill, chagrined. "And it wasn't done by von Stalhein—unless he's so clever he can be in two places at once."

"No. He went to the island. Someone came here in a plane—a light plane. It may not matter much, now that von Stalhein knows we're on the job, but whoever did this would see that another plane had been here. We also know *they've* got a plane. I must confess I'm a bit puzzled by this sudden rush to clean up every scrap of evidence. It's almost as if they knew I was on my way here. That could be so, of course. The enemy has spies everywhere, and just as I know von Stalhein's methods, he knows mine. Maybe that photo did it. Von Stalhein would realise that once it got into the papers he would almost certainly be spotted by our Intelligence people—as did, in fact, happen—and take steps accordingly. Well, it's not much use standing here staring at the ashes. I'm sorry, Bill, but I'm afraid your last piece of concrete evidence has gone up in smoke."

Bill, who had been on his hands and knees studying the footmarks, stood up. "There were three of 'em in the party that came here," he announced. "Pity I didn't bring my tracker along, or I could have told you more about 'em."

"You might measure the width of their wheel track while you're at it," requested Biggles. "As you know people by the size of their feet, I can sometimes name a plane by the span of its undercart."

Bill obliged. "Six foot, dead," said he.

"Auster," murmured Ginger.

"Could have been," agreed Biggles. "That would have the accommodation, but I'm not so sure about the endurance range. It must have come from a distance."

"The range of the new Auster, if I remember right, is six hundred miles," stated Ginger. "I know that isn't far as distances go here, but there was nothing to stop it from topping up its tanks at any airfield along the coast. It might even be doing that at Broome, at this moment."

"True enough," conceded Biggles. "We'll check up on that. If we knew where it refuelled, assuming it did, we should get a line on the direction it came from. If it didn't refuel then it can't be far away—unless it has a private petrol dump. Is there anything more you want to do here, Bill?"

"No."

"Then we might as well get along."

They took their places in the Otter and headed for Broome.

CHAPTER VII

OUTLOOK VAGUE

On arrival at Broome it was soon ascertained that no aircraft had refuelled there that day; but there was a message waiting for them. It was from Algy, to say he had arrived at Darwin, and had urgent news which, had he not turned up, West would have forwarded.

"Which is another way of saying that West has learnt something," remarked Biggles. "We'll push right on, Bill, if it's all the same to you. We should just make the trip in daylight."

"What about this light plane? Would you like me to check up along the coast to find out if a strange machine picked up petrol anywhere?"

"I'd be obliged if you'd do that," replied Biggles. "The information would be useful, whether the answer is yes or no. If it did, we should know which way it was travelling, and perhaps pick up some details about who was in it. If it didn't, then we should know that it's based no great distance away."

That concluded immediate affairs at Broome. Telling Bill that he would let him know any developments that concerned him, and asking him to send a signal to Darwin to let Algy know he was on his way, Biggles took off again on the six hundred mile run to the northern air terminal.

"If Algy's news is from West I can only think that West must have seen, or heard from, Alston," he opined—correctly, as it transpired. "It's a relief to know the Halifax is all right again because it begins to look as if we shall need it. At least, I assume it's all right. Algy wouldn't be such a fool as to start across the Timor Sea with a doubtful engine."

The run was made without incident, and from the air, in the rosy glow of the setting sun, the Halifax could be seen parked beyond the end hangar with Algy and Bertie standing beside it.

Biggles landed, taxied up alongside, switched off and jumped down, Ginger following. "Everything all right now?" was his greeting.

"Yes," confirmed Algy. "The trouble wasn't serious but I didn't feel like taking chances. West tells me you got my message. Any news?"

"Plenty," returned Biggles. "But let's have yours first; then we'll give you ours. We needn't stand here. With the weather as it is the machines might as well stay where they are for the night. Let's go over to the canteen. I've been on the go since daylight and I could drink a bucket of tea."

In the corner of the canteen, almost deserted at an hour when there were no arrivals or departures of aircraft, Algy explained why he had sent the urgent signal to Broome. The news, as Biggles had predicted, emanated from West. Briefly, it was this. Alston had arrived unexpectedly at Darwin the previous day, flying one of the regular services. He had spent the night there and then gone back to Brisbane, leaving before the Halifax had arrived; for which reason, of course, Algy hadn't spoken to him personally. However, Alston had given some information to West, who had passed it on.

"Is West on duty now?" put in Biggles.

"No. He's on night duty tonight. Comes on at ten."

"I see. Carry on."

Algy resumed. It appeared that Alston had seen a man named Smith on the airfield at Cloncurry some days earlier, in process of buying a second-hand aircraft that had been on offer there.

"Was it by any chance an Auster?" inquired Biggles.

Algy looked astonished. "Yes. An Auster Autocrat. How did you know?"

Biggles smiled faintly. "We've seen its footprints in the sand. "Go ahead."

Algy concluded his narrative. The Auster's registration was VH-NZZ. With Smith had been a younger man, a qualified pilot who had taken the machine up on a trial run. His name, according to the transfer papers, was Cozens. Alston didn't know him. In fact, he'd never seen or heard of him, although he thought he knew all the professional pilots in the country. When Alston, who was out on a job, returned to Cloncurry, the Auster had gone; no one knew where. Smith had paid for the machine and Cozens had flown it off, taking Smith with him. That was all.

Biggles tapped a cigarette on the back of his hand. "So

51

the gang has decided to get mobile," he observed.

"Who's this fellow Smith, anyway?" inquired Algy. "I'm in the dark. How did he suddenly pop into the picture?"

Biggles answered: "Smith is the name—or more probably the assumed name—of the chap who chartered the aircraft that collected von Stalhein and his pals from here when they disappeared. He was already in Australia and may turn out to be the big noise. Now he's bought an aircraft, which will save him using public transport."

"As we know its registration there should be no difficulty in locating it."

"Maybe not—always supposing it stays on public airfields," agreed Biggles. "But short of tearing round the continent ourselves looking for it how are we going to find out where it is? To call in the police, or the civil aviation authorities, would mean explanations and start the sort of hue and cry I'm anxious to avoid. This self-enforced security is really our big handicap. I mean, you couldn't have anything like an official search without von Stalhein getting to hear of it—and he'd know just what to do about that. But I'd better tell you and Bertie what has happened since we came here or we shall be talking at cross purposes. Things have moved faster than I expected."

For the next half-hour Biggles narrated the events since their arrival in Australia. "That's how things stand at present," he concluded. "Although we've learned quite a lot," he went on, "all it has really done is thicken the fog, and left me wondering just what it is we're trying to do. Chasing von Stalhein, or any other members of the gang, round the horizon, isn't going to get us anywhere, as far as I can see. Even if we caught up with them, what then? You can't arrest a man unless you have a case against him. There's no law against buying ships or aeroplanes. You can't prevent a man, in a free country, from cruising round the islands, or from sitting close enough to Woomera to hear the rockets go by—provided he behaves himself."

Bertie gave his monocle a rub. "In that case, old boy, would you mind telling me just what we're doing here? Sorry, and all that, but I don't seem to have got it."

"In a vague sort of way I can see two objectives," said Biggles. "The first is to find the headquarters of this man

Smith, and the other is to get a complete list of the names that were in that secret file, one page of which we found on the island."

"And then what?"

"I'd report back to the Air Commodore and suggest the whole thing should be handed over to the Australian Security people for any action they considered necessary. Obviously it would be out of the question for us to watch an unknown number of potential spies."

"Why not hand the case over as it stands?" suggested Algy. "Why did the Air Commodore start us on this will-o'-the-wisp hunt?"

"In the first place, I fancy he was actuated by the fact that von Stalhein was in the forefront of the scheme, and we know him and his methods. You must also bear in mind that the Air Commodore didn't know what we know now; or what we suspect; that the ramifications of this business are widespread. Anyway, having started I think we must go on. There are several lines that we could follow."

"What's the first," asked Ginger.

"Obviously, we must check on this lugger *Matilda* and see if we can establish how it comes into the set-up. That shouldn't be difficult. The owner must be on the gang's pay-roll or he would not have been taken to the island where Wada was murdered. Nor would he have tried to ram the Otter, with the intention, no doubt, of leaving us marooned on the island."

"But hold hard, old boy," interposed Bertie. "About this ramming effort. I know I'm a bit slow on the uptake, but I don't quite get it. According to Ginger, the wily Erich had a bunch of blacks with him. There were only two of you on the island. Why didn't he bump you off while he had the chance?"

"I can think of reasons why that might have been a silly thing to do," averred Biggles. "In the first place there was the aircraft. Had there been shooting Ginger could have taken off and radioed an S.O.S. for help; in which case the *Matilda*, on the high seas, wouldn't have had a hope of escaping interception. On top of that, don't forget Bill Gilson was in uniform. I might not have been missed, but Bill would have, and to murder a policeman, in this part of the world particularly, is to start something. For all von Stalhein knew Bill might have left word where he was going. No. Collision with the Otter, which would have left us stuck on the island, certainly long enough for the *Matilda* to reach the mainland, was safer. Had there been trouble it could be said the collision was an accident, and it would have been difficult to prove otherwise."

Ginger chipped in. "I had the feeling that Blackbeard, on the lugger, didn't like to act on his own responsibility. He waited for von Stalhein to get aboard—and Erich had already decided what to do."

"Which brings us to the question, what do we do next?" said Algy. "Wait here for the *Matilda* to come home?"

"Because *Matilda* is registered in Darwin it doesn't necessarily follow that she'll come here," Biggles pointed out. "After what's happened von Stalhein wouldn't be likely to overlook the probability of someone being here to meet him. When we've had something to eat I'll take a stroll along the water-front to see if I can pick up any gen about *Matilda* or her owner."

"What's the drill for tonight?" enquired Ginger.

"We'll go into the town to get a meal. A walk'll do us good."

"Taking our small-kit?"

Biggles hesitated. "I don't think so. I don't like sleeping too far away from the machines. A hotel usually means a delay in the morning. We'd be just as comfortable on our mattresses in the cabins, and on the spot to move off smartly in the morning should we decide to go somewhere. After we've had some food I'll go to the harbour. Don't wait for me. I'll join you here when I'm through."

One of the airport hands came into the canteen. He looked around, and called: "Mr. Bigglesworth here?"

"Over here," answered Biggles.

The man came over and handed him a folded slip of paper. "From the control room," he said, and walked away.

Biggles read the message. "It's from Bill Gilson. Good chap. Does what he says he'll do. This is interesting. Auster VH-NZZ refuelled at Wyndham eleven thirty-five hours. Pilot and two passengers. Came in from south-west. Left heading north-east."

"Which means it was coming this way," said Ginger.

"It didn't land here or we should have seen it," stated Algy.

"I wonder if we could find it," murmured Biggles,

reflectively. He got up. "Let's stretch our legs and see if we can find a beef-steak. That'll do to go on with."

CHAPTER VIII

THE OPPOSITION STRIKES BACK

LATER, after a good and satisfying meal, eight o'clock saw Biggles, by himself, making his way through the scented tropical night to the harbour, rubbing shoulders with as strange an assortment of humanity as could be found in any port on earth, east or west. Stockmen in sombreros; Chinese vendors of potato chips; pearlers; black boys on bicycles; Greek merchants, and seamen of every colour and race under the sun—Malays, Indonesians, Cingalese, Maoris, and Melville Islanders who had paddled their canoes across sixty miles of shark-infested water to go to the cinema and watch white screen stars doing things that must have been incomprehensible to them.

Biggles soon found what he was looking for, a public house where the customers appeared mostly to be Europeans—or part-European. He went in, and ordering a drink, was soon in conversation with an elderly man whose dress and speech made it clear that his business was connected with salt water. Presently, Biggles said casually: "You may be able to answer a question for me. There used to be a lugger here named *Matilda*. I don't see her now. Do you know what's happened to her?"

The man saw nothing odd in this question. "The *Matilda*," was the ready response. "Sure I know her. Used to belong to old Greeky Apergoulos. He sold her to that Dutchman Boller. Leastways he said he was a Dutchman, but I'd say he was a German. Don't see much of her now. They tell me Boller's working something up the Daly."

Biggles's muscles had tensed at the name Boller; and he was hard put to maintain his pose of indifference when it was followed by the word Daly; for he remembered, of course, that the two words went together on the list of names and addresses in his pocket. "Boller," he prompted. "Who was he? I don't seem to know him."

"You ain't missed much. Nobody here'd be sorry to see him go for good. Always looking for trouble. Went out of his way to find it."

"Was he a big fellow with a black beard?"

"That's him."

"You say he's doing something up the Daly."

"He's got a place at the head of the river. Cleaning a pandanus swamp to raise peanuts. So they say. I don't believe it. He never struck me as the peanut-growing sort. I know some fellers have done well at it, but it'd take more than peanuts to get me there. The Daly's no place for a Christian. Here it may be hell in the wet,* but up there, with every kind of biting bug making yer life miserable, blacks waiting for a chance to stick a spear in yer ribs, living on ironclads† and native tucker, it must be hell all the time. I ain't never been there, you understand, but I know some who have. Most of 'em stayed—for good."

Biggles was thinking fast. "Did you ever hear of a place up the Daly called the Flats?" he asked, although he was anxious not to arouse the man's suspicions by pushing his questions too hard.

"No, can't say as I have. But Taffy Walsh, over there, he'd know. He used to be on the old *Maroubra*, taking stores along and bringing down the nuts." Raising his voice the man called, "Taffy! Come over here." And when Taffy arrived he went on: "Here's a feller wants to know what it's like up the Daly."

The newcomer grinned. "Thinking of taking a holiday?"

Biggles smiled back. "No. Just interested."

"Like crocodiles?"

"I hate 'em."

"Then keep clear o' the Daly, 'cause scalies are thicker there than fleas on a dog's ear. I've seen a dozen or more eighteen-footers crowdin' on a few yards o' mud bank."

"He was askin' about a place called Daly Flats," said the first of Biggles's new acquaintances. "Ever hear of it, Taffy?"

"Yes. It's away up the top of the river; if I remember right, above where the Daly swings north towards Arnhem Land. If you want a spear in your gizzard that's the place to go."

"Are you serious? You really mean the blacks are

* Wet. The rainy season.   † Ironclads. Canned food.

bad?" queried Biggles, genuinely surprised, for he had supposed that dangerously hostile aborigines were a thing of the past.

"Not all of 'em; but them as are bad are as bad as they make up. Keep out o' their country. That's my advice."

The conversation lingered on a little longer, but as soon as he could break away without appearing discourteous, Biggles left the establishment, and well satisfied with his evening's work set about walking back to the airport. He had plenty to think about. Indeed, he had learned more than he expected. Outstanding, of course, was the surprising piece of information that the owner of the lugger was the Boller of Daly Flats, one of the names and addresses on the now important list. He was, apparently, reckoned to be an undesirable character even by Darwin standards, a port which, in its time, must have collected some tough types. Boller was believed to be a German. The man at Tarracooma Creek also had a German name—Roth. Adamsen, of Perth, might also be a German. It began to look as if the spy ring had been infiltrated from East Germany; or maybe von Stalhein and his associates had compiled a list of East Germans already domiciled in Australia. That was not to say, however, that they were active enemy agents. The Iron Curtain experts knew how to put pressure on unwilling, but sometimes helpless, persons. The scheme was beginning to take shape. Thus pondered Biggles as he strode on under a sky ablaze with stars, although occasionally they were partly blotted out by drifting masses of filmy cirro-cumulus cloud.

It was past ten o'clock when he reached the airport. The others would, he knew, be back by now, anxious to hear his news. Well, he had some to give them.

Walking past the hangars there was a minor incident which he was presently to remember, although at the time he didn't give it a second thought, the reason being, no doubt, that the possibility of personal danger, in Darwin, did not enter his head. He stopped to pass the time of night with a mechanic who had been working late in one of the sheds, and as they stood there chatting, the moon, which had been behind a cloud, rode clear.

It so happened, naturally perhaps, although without any conscious reason, Biggles was looking in the direction of the aircraft, and in the blue moonlight he saw, or thought he saw, an object move. What the object was he did not know. He couldn't remember seeing it before. It looked like a hump or something. Had he not gathered an impression that the thing had moved he would have taken it for a bag of freight, or mail, that had by an oversight been dropped and left out. It was as if the object had been moving, but froze into immobility at the precise moment the moon appeared. In the matter of distance it was between thirty and forty yards from the Otter. Not in the least degree concerned beyond the undesirability of having an animal wandering loose on the landing area, to the peril of planes coming in, he merely said to the mechanic: "What's that thing over there? Is it an animal or has somebody dropped something?"

The mechanic looked, but at that instant the moon was overtaken by another patch of drifting cumulus; and as the object could no longer be distinguished the question was allowed to pass. The mechanic, apparently more concerned about getting home, strode on towards the airport buildings. Biggles went on to the machines.

As he was soon to recall, he had yet another warning, although, still without the slightest suspicion of danger, he ignored it. As he drew close to the Otter, which was the nearer of the two machines, he glanced again at the "hump", and saw, with faint surprise, that it was not as far away as he had estimated. The distance was less than twenty yards; but he still could not make out what it was.

By this time he could hear the quiet murmur of voices inside the cabin, where the others were presumably together waiting for him, so he walked on to join them, and get a torch to examine the object that had puzzled him. Reaching the cabin door he turned to have a last look at it; and it was with a mild shock that he discovered that the thing, in some mysterious way, had not only closed the distance still more but had somehow flattened itself on the ground. Convinced now that it was an animal he took a pace towards it.

What followed occupied not more than three or four seconds of time.

The object, as black as night, leapt up. An arm went back, and Biggles realised for the first time that it was a man. Seeing that something was about to be thrown, he ducked instinctively. Almost simultaneously something swished over his head and struck the hull of the Otter with a crisp thud.

Biggles's reaction to the attack was to dart forward to seize his assailant; but the man twisted, and turning, raced away across the turf at fantastic speed, dodging and leaping in an extraordinary display of evading tactics. Pursuit was obviously futile. Biggles whipped out a pistol and got as far as raising it; but reluctant to alarm the aerodrome with gunshots he allowed his arm to drop, at the same time looking round to make sure the man had been alone. The moon reappeared. Not a soul was in sight.

Artificial light spread a yellow patch on the grass as the door of the cabin was thrown open. Algy's voice said: "That you, Biggles?"

"Yes," answered Biggles, somewhat breathlessly, for the suddenness of the attack had left him a trifle shaken.

"What's going on?"

"I don't quite know."

"What was that thud? Something hit the cabin."

"It thundering nearly hit me," said Biggles grimly. "Let's see what it was." Walking up to the hull he seized, and jerked free, a short, triple-barbed spear.

"For heaven's sake," came Algy's voice, aghast. "Did someone throw that at you?"

"Yes. A black. And if I hadn't come along, you, or the first person to open that door, would have got it. I saw the devil creeping up to the machine as I came along; but I wasn't expecting anything like this. He may have thought we were all inside. I don't know."

"He dropped something—or left it behind." Algy walked out a few yards and came back with a soft mass of something in his hands.

"What is it?" asked Biggles.

"Rag, or tow, or something of that nature. It's wet. My gosh! It's dripping with petrol."

"It looks as if the idea was to set fire to the machine. As they're so close, if one had caught fire the other would have gone too."

"And if the door had been jammed we should have been trapped inside."

A voice from the cabin cried: "Here, I say, you fellers, what's the flap?"

"Let's get inside," Biggles told Algy, in a hard voice.

59

In the cabin the others were told what had happened. "What do you make of it," asked Ginger.

"Obviously, somebody was hoping to get rid of us, or at least the machines. Which, equally obviously, means that that person knows we're here, and what we're doing."

"Von Stalhein."

Biggles shook his head. "No. He doesn't work like that. Besides, he must still be at sea. The thing that puzzles me about this is how it has happened so quickly. I don't think von Stalhein could have known we were here till he saw us at the island—wait a minute though! I've got it. The answer's simple. That lugger, the *Matilda*, is fitted with radio. Of course it would be: to enable it to keep in touch with its headquarters. If we accept that, then several things become plain. As I see it now, what happened was this; and I'm pretty sure I'm right. This morning, the first thing that would hit von Stalhein when he realised we were on the job with an Australian police officer, was the boat lying on Eighty Mile Beach. Up to that moment it wasn't worth bothering about. But now it could be an awkward piece of evidence. He knew perfectly well that if I hadn't already been to look at it I should most certainly do so, and check up on it. It had to be got rid of. He radioed his headquarters, or Smith's headquarters—call it what you like—to warn them. An aircraft—the Auster—was available. Some of the gang got into it, flew to the beach and burnt the boat. If that's correct then the Auster is being kept either in Western Australia or the Northern Territory. What happens next? Smith, or somebody, guessing that we would base ourselves on Darwin, decides that we'd be better out of the way; so he brings along a cut-throat to mop us up."

"Are you suggesting that he keeps a supply of black thugs on hand?" questioned Algy dubiously.

"From what I learnt tonight I see no reason why he shouldn't," came back Biggles. "I'd better tell you about that, because it all adds up."

Biggles then revealed what he had gathered at the harbour. "So you see, Blackbeard is Boller, one of the names on the list. He's a German who has a place at the headwaters of the Daly. In other words, Daly Flats. Ostensibly, he's been clearing ground for peanuts. What he's *actually* been doing, I suspect, is making a landing strip for an aircraft. Whites, I understand, are few and far between; but there, to Arnhem Land, have apparently retired those blacks who want no truck with white men. Some of them are bad medicine. So I'm told. I don't know. I've never been there. But as we may have to go we'd better check up on it. West must know the facts. He may be able to tell us the district where they use this type of spear—or put us on to somebody who can. He should be on duty now. I'll walk along and ask him."

"Here, watch what you're doing old boy," protested Bertie. "This beastly bodkin may not be the only one on the airfield."

"Don't worry," retorted Biggles grimly. "If anyone comes close enough to me to chuck one, he'll be the first to meet a piece of metal coming the other way. You watch the machines. From now on it means guard duty. Infernal nuisance; but not such a nuisance as trying to get a bunch of barbs out of your ribs."

"Well, chase Aunt Lizzie round the haystacks!" exclaimed Bertie. "This warrior stuff is all news to me. I thought the aborigines were generally pretty friendly."

"So did I," returned Biggles. "And so they usually are, except for—well, take a look at that spear. There's nothing friendly about that. I'll see what West has to say about it. I shan't be long."

Taking the spear, Biggles departed.

He was away about half an hour. When he returned the others looked at him expectantly as he held out the spear. "West says this thing came out of Arnhem Land. He asked me how I got it. When I told him he thought I was kidding. Said that sort of thing didn't happen here. I assured him that it did. He told me this top corner of Australia used to be called the triangle of death on account of the ferocity of the natives. Even today, with native reserves and all that sort of thing, they're not to be trusted. That goes for the half-civilised blacks who work up the Daly for the white planters. Incidentally, what struck me as odd—or significant if you like—was this. West said many of the early peanut farmers were Russians. I wonder does that mean anything. Any who are left would certainly employ some black labour. What I'm getting at is, that fellow who had a go at me couldn't have had any personal grudge against me. He could have had no possible reason for wanting to set fire to us, anyway. Somebody sent him; somebody who knows how to handle blacks."

Biggles was silent for a while, his expression hardening. "You know, that thought puts an uncomfortable notion into my head." He paused again, and continued: "After what West told me I'd decided to do a high reconnaisance over the headwaters of the Daly; but that can wait for a bit. There's no hurry. Airstrips don't run away. And the *Matilda* can't be back there yet, if that's where she's going. I'll tell you what. Tomorrow morning I shall run down to Broome in the Halifax and have a word with Bill Gilson. Ginger can come with me. Algy, you take Bertie with you in the Otter and see if you can spot the *Matilda*. Don't go near it. I'll give you a course from the mouth of the Daly River to the island. If, on that course, you see a lugger heading for the Daly it's pretty certain to be the *Matilda*. Get its position. That's all I want. Take the machine up to the ceiling: the moment you spot the lugger, cut your engines and turn away. It doesn't really matter if they see you, but it'd be better if they didn't. When you've done that make for Broome. We'll wait there for you."

"Okay," agreed Algy.

"It's getting late if we're to make an early start. I'll take first watch. The rest of you see about getting some sleep," concluded Biggles.

CHAPTER IX

MURDER IN THE OUTBACK

IT was still only nine o'clock the next morning when Biggles and Ginger arrived at Bill Gilson's house, just in time to catch him going out. The airport superintendent had promised to keep an eye on the machine.

Bill looked surprised to see them. "You fellers don't waste any time," he observed cheerfully.

"We've none to waste," returned Biggles, introducing Ginger. "Let's go into the office. I want a word with you."

"Now listen, Bill," he went on, when they were settled. "Has Joe Hopkins, your old prospector pal, come in yet?"

"No."

"You mentioned he was overdue."

"He is."

"Is that customary?"

"No. He's usually pretty regular. The tucker he takes with him lasts just so long and no longer. There's nothing to eat in the spinifex. If he isn't soon in I shall have to do something about it."

"Are there any blacks in the district he works?"

Bill stared. "What's that got to do with it?"

"Are there?"

"Yes. Plenty. But you needn't worry about that. He knows them and they know him."

"There's never any trouble with them?"

A curious expression dawned on Bill's face. "Now what made you ask that?"

"Last night, on Darwin airport, one tried to spear me."

Bill's expression turned to incredulity. "At *Darwin!* Are you pulling my leg?"

"There was nothing funny about it, believe you me," retorted Biggles seriously. "I have reason to believe that the man was an Arnhem Lander. I also have reason to believe that the people I'm looking for, which includes Boller, one of the names on that list I showed you, have an airstrip at the top end of the Daly. They've certainly got one no great distance away. That's where the Auster must have come from with the people who burnt the boat."

Bill shook his head. "There's nothing queer in Australia about a private airstrip. Everyone flies—farmers, stockmen, doctors, everybody—and thinks nothing of it. We were about the first people to become what used to be called airminded. No doubt it was a matter of the distances people had to cover to get anywhere. To be fifty or a hundred miles from your nearest neighbour is nothing in this part of the world."

Biggles nodded. "I realise that. But you still haven't answered my question about the general behaviour of the natives."

"Well, since you mention it, there have been reports of—well, if not exactly trouble—difficulties. Of course, some of 'em always have been awkward and unreliable; and lately, instead of getting more friendly, as you'd expect, there's been what you might call a stiffening in their attitudes towards white men. Old Harry Larkin —he's another old timer—told me the other day that a party on what they call walkabout had threatened him. I took it with a pinch of salt, although I must admit that Harry isn't the sort to be easily scared. But what's all this leading up to?"

Biggles lit a cigarette. "You'll call me an alarmist, I know, but it occurred to me last night that this is just how the trouble began in Malaya and Kenya."

When Biggles said that Ginger knew just when the thought had struck him, the previous evening, and he had paused in the middle of a sentence.

Bill was staring. "Do you mean Mau-Mau, and that sort of thing?"

"That's exactly what I mean."

Bill smiled sceptically. "But that couldn't happen here."

"Why couldn't it?"

"Well, it just couldn't, that's all."

"Tell me why."

"Most of 'em are in regular touch with whites."

"So they were in Africa."

"They've got their own reserves——"

"So they had in Africa."

Bill shook his head. "I still don't see how it could happen here."

"Neither, I imagine, could the settlers who took their wives and kids to outlying farms in Kenya, and now never move without a gun in each hand." Biggles went on. "Now look, Bill; I'm not the sort of man to get in a flap easily; and I own freely that I may be barking up a tree with nothing in it. I also own that when I came out here the last thing in my mind was trouble with the natives. I didn't really know what I *was* looking for. But since I've been here one or two things have happened that have made me think hard. Last night, after that man had flung a spear at me, the idea suddenly came to me that the set-up in the sparsely populated areas of Australia is exactly the same as in East Africa. Natives, without settled homes, outnumbering the whites. Isolated homesteads far apart. Stockmen, farmers and prospectors out on their own . . . It only needs one or two people to walk about telling the natives that white men are a lot of thieves who have swindled them out of their land, and turned them into slaves, and the next thing is murder." Biggles made a deprecatory gesture. "I may be quite wrong, but putting two and two together from what I've learnt since I came here, that was the ugly picture that suddenly crystallised in the fog. This dirty business is all part of the Cold War. It has worked in Malaya, Kenya, Indonesia, Burma and all over the Middle East, so I don't see why it shouldn't happen here. The men who landed in that stolen boat on Eighty Mile Beach came from behind the Iron Curtain, which is the general headquarters of the Cold War. I know more about them than you do. Whether I'm right or wrong about what they're doing here, don't kid yourself that they can't hurt *you*, or that the technique that has worked in Asia and Africa couldn't work in Australia." Biggles stubbed his cigarette.

Bill's expression had changed. "I never looked at it like that," he admitted soberly.

"Well, it might be worth your while if you bore it in mind and kept an ear to the ground for rumours of agitators. You told me yourself that this fellow Adamsen, in Perth, was known to be one."

"He's left Perth, they say."

"Oh he has, has he. I wonder what he's up to. And what about Roth, of Tarracooma Creek—wherever that might be."

"I've found out where that is."

"Where is it?"

"It's an old sheep run on the edge of the desert, south-east from here."

"How far?"

"Roughly, between a hundred and a hundred and fifty miles."

"Would Hopkins be in that direction?"

"More or less. He's not so far out, of course—mebbe forty miles."

"Would I be likely to fly over him if I went to Tarracooma?"

"Not unless you made a bit of a dog's leg."

"Might I see him from the air?"

"I should think so. He's got a mine—or rather, a digging—with a home made crusher. He lives in a wurlie, that's a bough shelter, near what we call a soak, to pro-

C

vide him with water. He scratches enough gold dust to keep him going."

"Do you know exactly where this place is?"

"Sure. I've called on him there. It's at the foot of the MacLaren Hills."

"This soak, as you call it. Would that be the only water supply in the district?"

"Yes."

"Would the natives use it?"

"I expect so."

"Then it might be a good thing if someone had a look to see if Hopkins is all right."

"He can take care of himself."

"I'm glad to hear it, because if Tarracooma is a prospective trouble spot, and being on my list it may be, the natives in that area may be some of the first to get restless."

"I see what you mean," replied Bill slowly.

Biggles glanced at his watch. "While I'm down here I think I'll run out and have a look at this place Tarracooma. I could take in Joe's workings on the way. Would you care to come along?"

"I would, very much."

"Okay. By the way, whether Joe is all right or not, I wouldn't say anything about my suspicions to anyone just yet. There may be nothing to it. But when a fire is smouldering it only needs one spark to set it alight. That's why I'm hoping you're right about Joe being able to take care of himself; because if he isn't that may be the spark."

"If he isn't, don't worry; I'll catch the man who did the mischief," said Bill grimly.

"Exactly," returned Biggles drily. "The result of that would be more trouble by way of a reprisal—and up goes the balloon. But let's not talk about that until we have to. Let's go."

They all walked briskly to the garage where Bill kept his car.

"If you'll keep low I shall be able to pick up my landmarks as we go along," he averred

Presently the Halifax, at a few hundred feet, was heading out over the inhospitable terrain that lies behind so much of Western Australia's coast. At the worst it was stark desert, with ribbed sand dunes and tawny hills; at

66

the best, spiky spinifex and salt bush. Salt lakes, as round as saucers, dotted the landscape, reflecting the clear blue of the sky. There was not a living creature in sight. This, brooded Ginger, was the true Australia, still the same as it had been for countless years before the white man came.

"Take a line on the dip between those two humps on the horizon—a bit to your right," requested Bill, and as Biggles altered course a trifle he resumed his scrutiny of the wilderness for the missing prospector.

The objective took on a more distinct outline as the machine droned on towards it; but of the missing man there was no sign. The scene remained as lifeless as a picture.

"Make for the bottom of the gulley in that hill on your right," said Bill. "There's a clump of mulga near it. It's just this side of it that Joe has his wurlie. You'll see the mine. He should be there, or not far away."

"He isn't there—unless he's deaf," said Biggles evenly. "If he was about he'd be looking at us by now."

The Halifax roared over the mine. Biggles circled it twice, losing height. A hole in the ground, the primitive bough-shelter, a billy-can hanging over a dead fire and some implements lying about, were all that could be seen.

"He should be there," muttered Bill. "He hasn't started for home. If he had he would have taken his billy with him."

"What do you suggest we do?"

"I'd like to go down and have a look. Can you land?"

"It ought to be possible on that bare flat area. Let's see."

Biggles flew on to the area of desert he had indicated. "Seems to be all right," he decided. "We'll try it. But don't blame me if we have to walk home."

Actually, the ground was level and devoid of vegetation, and Biggles put the aircraft down without much risk, finishing his run about three hundred yards from the prospector's lonely workings.

"The machine can't take any harm where it is," remarked Biggles, as they got out, and began walking towards the mine.

The sun was flaying the earth with bars of white heat that made the air quiver and the distant skylines shake; but everything else was still. There was no sound; no song of a bird, no whisper of a breeze. As they drew near the wurlie the silence seemed to take on a sinister quality; for it must have been evident to all that the miner was not there or he would certainly have shown himself by now. Maybe that was why Bill lengthened his stride so that he was the first to reach the shelter.

He took one glance inside, and the face that he turned to the others had lost its colour. "He's dead," was all he said.

The old prospector lay in a crumpled heap. He had obviously been dead for some days. There were some ugly black marks on the sand, on which the flies were busy.

"Stay where you are," said Bill, in a flat voice. "I'd better attend to this."

Biggles lit a cigarette and surveyed the sterile landscape.

"He was murdered," reported Bill, when he had finished his inspection. "Blacks. He was clubbed, and stabbed to death with spears. Couldn't have had a chance to defend himself. Came on him in the night, mebbe. Where's his rifle? I don't see it. I know he had one. Kept it in case he got a chance for a shot at a kangaroo. It was an old service .303. Had his initials on the butt, I remember. No cartridges, either. Queer."

"I see nothing queer about it," said Biggles. "When this sort of thing starts that's how it goes. The blacks probably killed him for his rifle. Now, perhaps, you see what I mean," he concluded, significantly.

Bill tipped his hat on the back of his head. "I still can't believe it. This sort of thing was common enough years ago but it doesn't often happen now—not in these parts, anyway. Poor old Joe. And to think how many times he shared his water and tucker with aborigines."

Biggles shook his head. "That doesn't always make much of a difference. If they need ammunition and weapons badly enough, they don't let anything stand in their way. More than one doctor has been murdered by the man he's just cured. What are you going to do about it?"

"We shall have to bury him. It's usual here to bury a perish, as we say, where he's found. We've tools. Then I'll fetch my tracker and see what he has to say about it."

"You mean, you'll follow up the murderers?"

"To hell and back if necessary. We don't let anybody,

black or white, get away with murder—not even here. Don't tread on more ground than you can help."

All taking a hand they dug a shallow grave. The body of the old digger was laid in it, after which the earth was replaced and stones piled on it. Bill recited the Lord's Prayer, stuck the spade in the ground at the head of the grave and started to collect the dead man's few simple belongings, putting them in his 'swag'—a coarse canvas holdall. After searching about for a little while in the wurlie he said: "There's something else missing."

"What is it?" asked Biggles.

"His dust—gold dust. He wouldn't have stayed here had his claim been worked out. He always managed to get a few ounces. Kept it in a little kangaroo-hide bag he made. I've seen it scores of times."

"He might have hidden it."

"Not he. Why should he? He wouldn't be expecting trouble."

"Seeing the blacks——"

"He had no time to hide it, even if he thought of it, which isn't likely. From the way he was killed he hadn't time to do anything."

"Then if it isn't here the murderer must have taken it."

Bill nodded. "That's the only answer." He fastened the swag and picked it up. "That's the lot," he said, and turned to go, only to stop dead, leaning forward, like a dog pointing game.

Ginger did not have to look far for the reason. A hundred yards away a score of naked aborigines were standing in a group, watching them. All carried spears. To say that he was astonished would be to put it mildly. How, and from where, the blacks had appeared in a scene that he would have sworn was lifeless, was a mystery.

"Now what?" murmured Biggles.

"I'll have a word with 'em. It may be the mob that murdered Joe."

"You know more about it than I do, but I'd say not," replied Biggles. "The mob that killed Joe, knowing what was bound to follow, would surely make themselves scarce."

"We'll see." Bill started walking purposefully towards the blacks, who remained as rigid as if they had been carved in stone. "If they didn't do the killing they'll know all about it."

"Have you got a gun?" queried Biggles.

"I don't need one."

Biggles shrugged. To Ginger he said quietly: "There are times when fearlessness can be foolish. If I know anything about natives, that bunch is all keyed up to jump. They themselves, with their simple minds, don't know yet which way they'll go. They may run. If they don't, anything can happen."

Bill stopped at a distance of about twenty yards. "What name?" he shouted.

There was no answer, no movement.

"Which way country belong you?" demanded Bill.

No answer.

"What yabber-yabber belong you," persisted Bill. "You been savvy what happen longa here."

The blacks remained like graven images, their dark eyes unwinking, on the policeman.

"Listen, Ginger," said Biggles tersely, "He's not going to do anything with that lot, and if he tries there's going to be trouble. Make for the machine. Start up. You may be able to bring it nearer. Behave as if nothing is happening. Above all, don't look scared."

"Okay." Ginger started off for the machine, which was not directly behind them but at an angle between the two parties, so that he was able to watch events out of the corner of his eye.

Biggles with his hands in his pockets, was strolling nearer to Bill as if nothing was going on. Coming within earshot he said: "I don't think that's your lot, Bill. I don't see a rifle."

"The devils won't talk."

"If they've decided to take that line you won't make 'em. Push them too hard and we're going to have casualties. We don't want that at this stage."

'I've never seen them in this mood before," came back Bill, in a voice tense with chagrin.

Biggles realised the position Bill was in. To retire now would look like weakness, loss of face. To go on was to invite open hostility. "You please yourself what you do; it's your country and you know best," he said, and lit another cigarette.

The Halifax's engines came to life and the big machine moved slowly and ponderously towards the opposing parties.

70

Said Bill, reluctantly: "I suppose you're right, but I hate letting 'em get away with it." He half turned.

The movement might have been the signal for which the blacks were waiting. While Bill's eyes were on them, like animals, they hesitated to do anything; but the instant he turned, they acted. With shrill whistles and strange cries they began to fan out.

Bill stared. Not only was he obviously surprised by this behaviour but it was evident that he still had not grasped what was unpleasantly obvious to Biggles; that their lives were in danger. Familiarity with natives normally friendly, had, no doubt, bred contempt, as was understandable. He refused to be intimidated, and it was with reluctance that he moved unhurriedly with Biggles towards the machine.

At the last minute a spear was thrown. It did no harm. But it so enraged Bill that Ginger, who was watching from the cockpit, thought that he was going for the thrower; a course that looked, and probably would have been, suicidal. Biggles had a pistol but he had not drawn it, presumably hoping to avoid hostilities. In any case it would not have been much use against the mob, had they charged.

Ginger decided to take matters into his own hands. Advancing the throttle, as the machine responded he swung it round so that the tail pointed at the aborigines. The result can be imagined. On the tearing slipstream of the four powerful engines a wall of dust, sand and dead vegetation, struck them like a tidal wave, and for a moment engulfed them. The stuff may well have stung their exposed bodies. At all events, it was more than they could face, and presently vague figures, hands over eyes, could be seen staggering about as they sought to get out of the blast.

Biggles and Bill took the opportunity to get aboard and the immediate danger was past. Ginger relinquished his seat to Biggles, who said, "Well done." He did not take off at once, but turning to Bill, asked: "Now what do you want to do? Do you want to go back to Broome or shall I go back to Tarracooma?"

"I'd rather get back to Broome," answered Bill. "Whether it suits your book or not I shall have to report the murder of Joe Hopkins, and the behaviour of those

71

lunatics outside. I can't think what the deuce has come over them."

."I can," murmured Biggles. "I hate saying I told you so, but I did try to give you an idea of what we might expect. We've got to work fast, Bill, or Joe Hopkins won't be the only man to perish. I'll take you home."

Leaving the naked warriors watching from a distance the Halifax roared into the air.

CHAPTER X

CLAWS OUT AT TARRACOOMA

THEY got back to Broome to find the Otter there, just in. Algy said they had spotted the *Matilda* about seventy miles out, on a course for the mouth of the Daly.

"That's what I expected, and all I want to know about it for the time being," said Biggles. He introduced Algy and Bertie to Bill, and then told them the result of their morning's work. "I'm pretty certain now that whatever else von Stalhein's associates are doing in Australia part of their job is to unsettle the aborigines. Aside from any material damage the blacks may do it tends to focus attention on them, which, of course, by employing police and aircraft, makes things easier for the spy ring to operate. How many full-blooded blacks have you got in Australia, Bill?"

"As near as can be judged, about fifty thousand. In addition, there are a lot of mixed breeds."

Bill grimaced. "Enough to do a lot of mischief."

"Those we saw this morning were Peedongs; they wander about the open country," explained Bill. "They're different from the jungle types you find in the Territory, called Myalls. They're all pretty wild, but the Arnhem Landers are the worst. Until recently it was almost certain death to go near them."

Biggles nodded. "If, as it seems, somebody has been working on the Peedongs to antagonise them, we can expect the same conditions in the Territory. In Western

Australia the trouble may have started at Tarracooma. In the Territory, up the Daly." He looked at Bill seriously. "I realise that you'll have to report the killing of Joe Hopkins, and try to find the murderer; but while you're doing that the trouble may spread. I imagine Hopkins wasn't the only lone prospector out in the wilds."

"Not by a long chalk. Some fellows work alone, others in pairs. And there are homesteads right off the map."

"They ought to be warned. The question is how to do it without starting a scare—and being laughed at for alarmists. And while people are laughing, the propaganda agents, realising that their racket has been rumbled, will work all the harder to set things alight. There's no time to lose. This ugly weed has got to be nipped in the bud. You can see how I'm fixed. I've no authority here to arrest anyone, even if I had a definite charge against him, which I haven't—yet."

"I might get the fellow who killed Hopkins. I've a good tracker."

"And while you're looking for him more murders may be committed. You might even be murdered yourself."

"What do you suggest I do?"

"What do you suggest *I* do? Of course, I could go to Sydney and see one of your Security people whose name has been given me; but that would take time, and it would certainly be some time before anything was done. I should have to convince the man that I wasn't talking through my hat, and he'd have to get instructions before he could take action. All the evidence I have would rest on my unsubstantiated word, and I feel that isn't enough. What I *really* want to do is have a sight of this mystery man Smith, who I suspect is at the root of the trouble. But he's outside your province." Biggles thought for a moment. "In view of what's happened I feel inclined to take the bull by the horns and tackle this fellow Roth at Tarracooma. That might stop the rot in this area."

"How?"

"You could arrest him, and bring him here for questioning."

"And make myself a laughing stock?"

"That, I must admit, is a chance you'd be taking," conceded Biggles. "It's up to you to decide whether it's worth risking your career to save some of your people out there in the blue without a thought of danger in their

73

heads. There is, of course, a possibility that Roth, if he's a guilty party, may panic when he sees us, and do something that would warrant your picking him up. We might find something incriminating in his house. Anyway, it would be worth while if we could force him to hold his hand while I got cracking on Daly Flats."

Bill looked worried, as he had every reason to be. "This is a free country," he argued. "A man can go where he likes and do what he likes as long as he doesn't break the law. And there's no law against talking, to blacks or whites."

"And that's exactly what the enemy reckons on," declared Biggles. "It makes his job easy and ours difficult. Well, I'm going to Tarracooma. You can please yourself whether you come or not."

"I'll come with you," decided Bill. "We could have a look at this feller Roth. No harm in that. On the way I could see what aborigines were on the move. Give me a minute to report Hopkins's murder and I'll be with you."

"What about us," queried Algy, while they were waiting.

"You and Bertie can come along. Anything can happen, and the more witnesses we have the better. The Otter will be all right here."

"How do you know you'll be able to land at Tarracooma?" inquired Bill, when he returned.

"I don't know. But it's my guess there will be some sort of landing facility. Roth may be only a small fish in the spy outfit but his boss would want to keep in contact with him; and unless I'm off my mark his boss is Mr. Smith, who has an aeroplane. Do you think you'll be able to find the place, Bill?"

"I know the general locality. It's unlikely that there's more than one establishment there, so if we see one, that should be it."

In a few minutes the Halifax was in the air again, on a course a little more to the south than last time. The same sort of country lay below, although there were wide areas of absolute desert, sand or "gibbers", the rounded stones that look as if they should be on a seaside beach. Later there were broad patches of mulga—a small tree shrub of the acacia family. From one such growth a thin column of smoke was rising. Presently Biggles noticed another, and asked: "What's that smoke? I don't see anyone about."

Answered Bill: "We call 'em mulga wires. Or if you like, bush telegraph. Blackfella talk. Natives signalling."

"About us?"

"Possibly. Or about the murder. When you're on the ground everyone gets advance notice that you're on the way. But I doubt if the smoke signals can travel as fast as a plane. In the ordinary way I'd say they have no special significance; but I don't like the way the blacks are keeping out of sight. Of course, if they know a white man has been killed that could be enough to send them into hiding. They know jolly well that someone will have to pay for it."

The aircraft droned on. The only sign of life in the wilderness was a small mob of kangaroos.

"We call that light scrub and sand country ahead, pindan," informed Bill. "If this Tarracooma outfit is really raising sheep we soon ought to see something of 'em. A sheep run can have a frontage of a hundred miles."

The Halifax droned on, bumping badly in the shimmering heat.

Another twenty minutes passed and Bill said: "Tarracooma should be about here somewhere. It's new ground to me so I can't say exactly where it is. There's pretty certain to be a billabong—that's a waterhole—so if you climbed a bit higher, and circled, we might spot the light shining on it. Water stands out clear in this sort of country. If there isn't any natural water there should be an iron windmill working an artesian well."

As it turned out there was a waterhole. As Biggles climbed Ginger spotted it a long way off. He called attention to it, whereupon Biggles cut the engines and began a long glide towards it. Some buildings, made conspicuous only by the shadows they cast, came into view; and a few sheep. Then one or two blacks appeared, running; one led two horses into a building, presumably a stable.

"I can see wheel marks on that sand patch," said Bill.

"So can I—but there's nothing to show what made them," replied Biggles. "Could have been a car, although they look a bit too wide for that. We shall soon see. You'd better do the talking. What line are you going to take?"

75

"The first thing is to have a look at Roth, and see how he shapes."

"You'll have to give a reason for calling."

"I'll ask him if he's had any trouble with his black boys."

"He'll say no. Which as far as he's concerned will probably be true, because he's one of the very people who's causing the trouble. At least, I think he must be. I can think of no other reason why he should be on von Stalhein's list."

"I shall bear that in mind," asserted Bill.

The range of buildings was now almost directly below. The actual house was a long low bungalow of timber and corrugated iron. Ginger thought it looked new. Certainly it had not been there very long.

"No one's come out to have a look at us," observed Bill.

"They're looking all right, don't make any mistake about that," returned Biggles, with a suspicion of a sneer in his voice.

He landed down a rather confused line of tracks and ran on as near the bungalow as was practicable, the distance from it being about fifty yards. He switched off. They got down. Ginger could see blacks watching them surreptitiously from the outbuildings.

"Somebody had better stay with the machine," decided Biggles. "In fact, I think you, Algy, and Bertie, might both stay. You'll be able to see what happens, and you'll be close enough to step in if Mr. Roth starts chucking his weight about. I don't think he will, but one never knows."

Bill, with Biggles and Ginger, strode on to the front door of the building; but before they reached it, it was opened, and a man stood on the threshold. The colour of his skin was enough to reveal at a glance that he was a mixed breed."

"Mr. Roth at home?" began Bill, casually.

"He is. I'm Roth," was the answer.

For a moment Bill looked somewhat taken aback. As, indeed, was Ginger, and no doubt Biggles too. Naturally, it had been assumed that Roth was a white man. That this was clearly not so put an unexpected factor into the proceedings; but there was of course no opportunity to discuss it.

"May we come in?" questioned Bill, cheerfully, for

they had received no invitation to enter. He moved forward.

With some reluctance, it seemed to Ginger, Roth gave way. He gave the impression that he, too, had been caught unprepared—unprepared, that is, for a visit from a police officer. Had Bill been travelling on foot, or on a horse, Roth would probably have had ample warning of his approach.

The door opened directly into what was plainly the living-room. The table was littered with dirty plates and glasses, more than one man would be likely to use at one meal. An empty whisky bottle stood amongst the debris.

"I see you're having a party," said Bill, evenly. "I hope I haven't disturbed it?"

This was spoken as a question; but Roth ignored it. "What do you want?" he asked, in a guttural voice that suggested, as did his name, German parentage on the white side of his pedigree.

"I'm calling on some of the people in the outback, to see if everything's going on all right."

"Why shouldn't it?"

"One or two of 'em report a little trouble with their black fellas."

"No trouble here."

"Who have you got in the house?"

"What's that got to do with it?"

"It just struck me that if you've got neighbours here I could speak to them while I'm on the ground. That would save me a journey, mebbe."

"What visitors would be likely to come here?"

"I don't know. You'd know better than me. I notice one of your friends has a plane."

Whether this was a shot in the dark, or whether Bill had mentally measured the wheel tracks outside, Ginger did not know. Bill knew the track of the Auster was six feet, for they had told him so on Eighty Mile Beach.

"Friend of mine come up from Perth," announced Roth, after a momentary hesitation, in which, apparently, he had decided not to deny that a plane had been there. Not that he could very well deny it, with the tracks outside.

"Would I know him?" asked Bill, carelessly.

"Shouldn't think so."

77

"What's his name."

Roth frowned. "Say, what's the idea of all these questions?"

"I'm just setting my clock right as to who's about in my territory. Have you some objection to answering a few civil questions?"

"Course not."

"Then why not tell me this man's name?"

Roth scowled. "All right. If you must know, it's Adamsen."

Biggles caught Ginger's eye.

"Is he still here?" asked Bill.

"Yes."

"Anyone else?"

Roth's scowl deepened. "Why should there be anyone else?"

Bill's manner did not change. "Only that I notice five people have just had a meal, and I reckon it'd take more than two of you to empty a bottle of whisky."

That did it. "What's it got to do with you who I have in my house?" spat Roth. "Ain't you got nothin' better to do than waste my time with a lot of fool questions? What are you trying to get at, anyhow?"

Bill's voice took on a more brittle quality. "What I'm trying to get at is the man who murdered Joe Hopkins, the digger."

Roth stiffened. Alarm showed for a moment in his eyes. He was not a good dissembler.

"So you knew about that," pressed Bill.

"I didn't say so."

"But you knew about it."

"No I didn't."

Bill strode to a corner of the room, picked up a rifle that was leaning against the wall, and holding it by the muzzle pushed the butt forward. "If you didn't know, how did this get here?" he rasped.

Roth stared. His tongue flicked nervously over his lips.

"This is Joe's rifle and you know it," challenged Bill.

"I didn't know who it belonged to," shouted Roth.

"How did it get here?"

"I took it off one of my boys."

"Why?"

"Because I won't let 'em carry guns."

"Then let's ask *him* where he got it from," said Bill firmly. "Send for him."

"He ain't here any longer," muttered Roth.

"Why not?"

"I sacked him a week ago."

"What was his name?"

"Charlie."

"Charlie what?"

"How would I know? I can't remember the name of every binghi who works for me."

"How many have you got working for you?"

"About a score."

"What do they all do?"

"What do binghis usually do on a station?"

"Look after the stock—when there is any," rapped out Bill, meaningly.

At this juncture the door of an inner room was opened and four men entered. One, the leader, was white; a cadaverous fellow with small dark eyes set close together and a straggling beard. Two were mixed breeds of questionable ancestry although one of them had more than a suspicion of Asiatic in his make-up. The other was a full-blooded aborigine, dressed like the rest.

"What's all the fuss about," inquired the leader of the newcomers.

"The fuss is about a murder," answered Bill, shortly. "Who are you?"

"The name's Adamsen—if that means anything to you." The man grinned unpleasantly, showing a row of broken discoloured teeth, as if he would make a joke of the business. "I ain't murdered anyone—so far," he added.

"I didn't say you had," retorted Bill curtly. He took out his note-book. "I'll have the names of the rest of you while I'm here," he stated. "I may have to call on you as witnesses."

A sullen silence settled on the room.

"Come on," requested Bill, impatiently, pencil in hand. No one answered.

"I see," said Bill, coldly. "So that's how you feel about it. Don't worry, I'll remember your faces. Is there anyone else in that room?" A few quick strides took him to the doorway through which the men had entered. After a glance round he said: "You got a licence for a wireless transmitter, Roth?"

"I ain't had time. It's only just been put in."

"Who put it in—Adamsen?"

There was no answer.

Bill came back. "You're coming with me," he told Roth.

"Where to?"

"Broome."

"Like heck I will. What for?"

"To make a statement as to how the property of a dead man came into your possession."

"I've told you all I know."

"I'm not satisfied with your explanation."

"It's as much as you'll get out of me. And I ain't moving from here."

"You won't gain anything by resisting the police."

"That's all you know," sneered Roth, apparently gaining confidence from the presence of his supporters.

At this point, before anyone could stop him, the black dodged across the room to the front door, and putting his fingers to his mouth let out a shrill whistle. Instantly, from where they had been watching, a score of blacks came running towards the house.

"I reckon it's time you were going," scoffed Roth.

Bill's lips came together in a hard line. "You rat, to drag these poor fellows into trouble."

Roth's grin broadened. "It's you that's in trouble, mister," he mocked. "Better get going."

"Yes, I'm going, and you're coming with me," said Bill, calmly—surprisingly calmly, Ginger thought, considering he was unarmed.

Roth's right hand began to move slowly towards his side pocket; but it stopped when he found himself looking into the muzzle of Biggles's gun.

"Don't move, anybody," said Biggles, with ice in his voice. "Ginger, give Bill your gun, then take the valves out of that radio equipment."

Ginger handed his gun to Bill and walked to the open door of the inner room. Adamsen half turned as if he would stop him.

Biggles's gun whipped round. "Stand still," he grated; and there was something in his manner that brought the man to an abrupt halt, staring.

80

Ginger went on. He was soon back. "Okay," he said.
"You'll pay for this," stormed Roth.

"We'll talk about who's going to pay later," said Bill.
"Are you coming with me?"

"No."

Bill handed his gun to Ginger. "Hold this," he said, in
a matter-of-fact voice. Turning back to Roth he put out
a hand to take his arm—or that was what it looked like.
At the same time he said: "For the last time, are you
coming quietly?"

"I'll see you in hell first," snarled Roth, and struck
Bill's arm aside.

Bill's fist flew out. It landed on Roth's jaw and hurled
him staggering back against the wall. Before he could
recover, moving at a surprising speed for a man of his
stature, Bill followed up and hit him again, this time
knocking him down. He stooped swiftly. Handcuffs
clicked. "I'll teach you to have a little more respect for
the law," he said trenchantly. "Come on."

All this had happened so quickly that the other members of the party hadn't moved, but stood staring, as if
finding it difficult to believe their eyes. Biggles, gun in
hand, watched them without emotion.

Ginger, wondering why the blacks did not come in,
threw a glance at the outside door. Algy was standing on
the step. The blacks had stopped before his automatic.

Bill, grim-faced, and a trifle pale under his tan, pushed
Roth towards the door.

Roth, seeing that his friends were not going to help
him, flew into a passion. In a voice thin with panic he
shouted: "Gimme a hand some of you. What are you
gaping at, you blasted cowards. Charlie——" He broke off
abruptly, as if realising that in his temper he had let
something slip.

Bill stopped. "Charlie," he repeated, and swung round
to face the aborigine, who was backing into the room.
"So you're Charlie?"

"Yes, he's Charlie," spat Roth vindictively. "I'm not
swinging for him."

Charlie moved like lightning. He whipped out a knife.
His arm went up.

Biggles hardly moved. His gun crashed. Charlie staggered screaming, clutching his arm. The knife clattered

on the floor. Biggles kicked it aside and grabbed the man by the scruff of the neck.

"Mind he hasn't got a gun in his pocket," warned Bill.

Biggles tapped the man's pockets. Apparently he felt something, for his hand dived into a side pocket. It came out holding a small but bulging bag of kangaroo hide.

"That's it," cried Bill. "That's Joe's poke. Bring him along."

"You won't want me now," contended Roth.

"You knew all about it," snapped Bill. "I'm holding you for an accessory."

Charlie was groaning. Whether Adamsen and the two half-breeds knew about the murder was questionable. At all events, they were clearly unwilling to be associated with it, for they did nothing. Roth was cursing Charlie luridly for keeping Hopkins' gold, about which he had evidently not been told. Altogether, it was an ugly example of crooks ratting on each other.

"You'll have to give me a minute to fix this man's arm," Biggles told Bill. "Get me some rag, Ginger. A towel will do. You'll probably find one in the kitchen."

There was a delay of a few minutes while a temporary bandage was put on the man's arm. When the job was done Biggles said: "Go ahead, Bill."

Carrying Hopkins' rifle Bill took his prisoners through the door. Ginger went with him. Algy was still covering the blacks. Biggles was last out of the house. He shut the door behind him.

There were a few critical moments with the blacks outside. They stirred uneasily and it looked as if they might attempt a rescue; but in the end they did nothing. Maybe it was Bill's uniform that made them hesitate to act. Perhaps it was the old story of everyone leaving the first move to someone else. The fact remains, they stood their ground, wide-eyed and open-mouthed as their primitive brains strove to keep pace with these unusual events.

The Halifax's engines started. Bertie left them idling and reappeared at the cabin door. Bill pushed his prisoners forward to him, and having handed them over turned about and deliberately walked back to the aborigines. What he said to them couldn't be heard for the noise of the motors. He made no threatening gestures; he carried no weapon, so the result seemed to be a good example of dominant will-power. The tension relaxed. One of them seemed to be explaining something. At the finish, when Bill dismissed them with a wave, they merely walked away.

"Wouldn't do to let 'em think we were scared of 'em," he remarked, when he rejoined the others. "I told 'em not to listen to anyone who came along trying to stir up trouble; and if they had any complaint, to make it to me, or the government Protector of Aborigines. Let's get along home."

Biggles went through to the cockpit, and two minutes later Tarracooma was dropping away astern in a haze of dust.

"What about Adamsen, and that other pair in the house?" asked Ginger.

"There was nothing we could do with them," answered Biggles. "They won't do anything. In fact, without their wireless, I don't see that there is much they can do. One thing they will do is think, and think hard. In the first place it must have given them a shock to know we're wise to their game. On top of that they learned about the murder, which I fancy was news to them. It was probably true that Adamsen came up from Perth to fix their wireless. Anyway, we've drawn their teeth for the time being, and that gives us breathing space to decide on our next move."

The Halifax droned on, kicking the thin desert air behind it.

CHAPTER XI

MOVE AND COUNTERMOVE

THE afternoon was still young when the Halifax got back to Broome, so Biggles, saying he had thought things over on the way, announced his intention of pushing straight on to Darwin with both machines. With Adamsen at Tarracooma there was no point in going to Perth, as he had at one time contemplated; and there was nothing more for them to do at Broome. Bill could be left to deal with the prisoners through ordinary routine channels. This he said he would do, for the time being withholding any reference to the general animosity of the aborigines which, after what had happened at Tarracooma, might fizzle out of its own accord without further trouble.

So after a cup of tea and a snack, thanking Bill for his efficient co-operation, the crews got into their aircraft and flew back together to Darwin without anything of interest happening on the way. As they had to pass over the mouth of the Daly River without deviating from their course they looked for the *Matilda*, but saw nothing of her. As a matter of detail there were several craft on the open sea, but they did not go down to investigate them, Biggles remarking that by this time the lugger was no doubt on the river. This was perhaps a natural assumption; but before long Biggles was to blame himself for assuming too much without supporting evidence.

During the run, he and Ginger discussed the general situation. Ginger was able to tell Biggles that the radio equipment at Tarracooma was very high frequency which pretty well confirmed Biggles's belief that Smith, or whoever the senior member of the spy gang might be, was in direct touch with his operatives regardless of distance. It was some satisfaction to know that as Tarracooma had been silenced it would be several days before he knew what had happened there. He might, Biggles thought, send the Auster down to find out.

The chief topic of conversation was what to do next. It was a problem that presented difficulties. Biggles said he was anxious to have a look at Daly Flats, from the air if not from the ground. But if that was to be done it ought to be done at once, before the lugger got there. He was equally anxious to see Colonel MacEwan, the Australian Security Officer at Sydney, for he felt that the time had come to put their cards on the table. They could not, he asserted, go on tearing about Australia, doing things which, if it was held that they had over-stepped their authority, might embarrass everybody concerned. At Tarracooma, by taking a chance and having Bill with them, all had gone well, and they had nipped off one of the ends of the spy network. They couldn't hope to go on doing that sort of thing without the Australian government asking them what the dickens they thought they were up to; and in any case the damage they had done would soon be repaired by Smith, who would carry on with his work.

As he had said before, Biggles went on, what he really wanted was the complete list of enemy agents in the country—or at any rate, those with whom von Stalhein was in touch, or had intended to get in touch on his arrival in Australia. That a duplicate list existed was not to be doubted. Who had it? Possibly Smith, who was certainly a senior member of the spy organisation if not the actual head. He now had his own plane for easy transport. It followed, therefore, that where the plane was, so Smith would be. And the most likely place for it to be at that moment, averred Biggles, was at Daly Flats, awaiting the arrival of the *Matilda*, so that Smith could learn at first hand from von Stalhein what had happened on the island. But once he had that information it was unlikely that he would stay there. Taking von Stalhein with him in the Auster, he would depart for an unknown destination. Hence the urgency.

"So you see," concluded Biggles, "if I go to Sydney to see Colonel MacEwan, the Security man whose name the Air Commodore gave me, I'd probably miss the boat—or rather, the plane—at Daly Flats. We should then be faced with the job of hunting the whole of Australia for the Auster. All this, of course, is assuming that Smith is at Daly Flats at this moment with the Auster."

"The Australian government would soon locate the Auster," declared Ginger confidently.

"I'm not so sure of that," returned Biggles. "Smith may keep clear of public airfields. For all we know he may have a dozen hide-outs like Tarracooma, or, as I suspect, Daly Flats."

"Does this Australian Security Officer know we're here?" queried Ginger.

"I'd say yes, although I haven't confirmed it. But I'm pretty sure the Air Commodore would let him know what was in the wind."

"Then as you can't go to Sydney *and* Daly Flats why not ring him up?"

Biggles shook his head. "Fancy trying to explain all this over the phone! Aside from that, on a public telephone service you never know who's listening."

The debate was resumed later, when they were all on the ground at Darwin, parked as before just beyond the end hangar. By the time they had topped up their tanks it was too late to do any more flying that day. Biggles gave his views as he had given them to Ginger, and the upshot of it all was, he resolved to go to Sydney, in the Halifax, starting at daybreak. The others, in the Otter, could make a cautious reconnaissance of the Daly Flats area, the main objectives being a possible airstrip, the Auster, and the position of the lugger, which, it was supposed, would by that time be well up the river. Having done this the Otter would return to Darwin, there to await Biggles's return.

Biggles said this plan did not entirely please him, but as he couldn't be in two places at once he could think of no alternative. His decision rested on the conviction that they couldn't go on tearing about the continent at the risk, should anything go wrong, of upsetting the Australian government, to say nothing of the government at home.

In pursuance of this plan it was agreed that they should have a meal at the airport and sleep in the machines. Biggles would have a word with West to see if he had any fresh news. In view of the attempt to burn the machines on the previous occasion when they had slept on the airfield it would be necessary to maintain an all-night guard, and the details of this disagreeable duty were arranged, it falling to Ginger's lot to take first watch.

"I don't like leaving the machines unattended even in daylight, so I think Ginger it would be best if you went and had your meal now," said Biggles. "We'll go when you come back."

"Fair enough," assented Ginger, and set off forthwith. It was still broad daylight although the sun was well on its way down to the horizon. There might be, he thought, three-quarters of an hour of daylight left.

With no other thought in his head than to get a meal as quickly as possible he strode on to the tea-room, which, he found, while not full was fairly well patronised. Some of the airport staff were there, a few air crews, and one or two civilians who he supposed were waiting for the Qantas liner due in shortly from Singapore. His eyes ran over them as he pulled out a chair to sit down, more from habit than any expectation of seeing a person he knew.

Suddenly he stopped dead. Then he pushed the chair back into place, turned about and left the room. For a little way, in order not to attract attention to himself, he walked on; but as soon as he was clear of the building he ran. The others must have seen him coming, for by the time he reached the Otter, in the cabin of which he had left them, Biggles had opened the door and stood waiting.

"What's wrong?" asked Biggles quickly.

"Von Stalhein's in the tea-room," answered Ginger breathlessly—the breathlessness not being entirely due to exertion.

Biggles looked incredulous. Not for a long time had Ginger seen him so taken aback. But he recovered quickly. "Is he alone?" he asked, jumping down.

"I think so. He was sitting alone at a table. I didn't stop to check up."

"Doing what?"

"Looking out of the window as if he was expecting somebody. There were tea things on the table."

"Did he see you?"

"No—but I wouldn't swear to it. I turned my back as soon as I saw him. I wasn't expecting——"

"Neither was I," cut in Biggles shortly.

"Well, blow me down!" exclaimed Bertie from the door. "That blighter is a fair corker. How the deuce did he——"

"Just a minute—let me think," interposed Biggles curtly. "This is what comes from taking things for granted. Either the *Matilda* didn't go up the river but came to Darwin instead, or else von Stalhein was put ashore at Wyndham and came up on the regular service. The plane came in from the south while we were sitting here talking."

"The lugger was heading for the mouth of the Daly when I last saw it," declared Algy. "Bertie will confirm that."

"It could have had its course changed by wireless."

"But why should von Stalhein come here?"

"For the reason most people go to an airport, I imagine," answered Biggles drily. "To catch a plane. You realise that this has knocked my plan sideways. No matter. Let's get things in line. Von Stalhein can't know we're here or he'd hardly be sitting in a public room. We were already here when the plane from the south landed, so if he was on it it's unlikely he'd notice our machines. Or put it the other way round. Had he been here when we landed he would have seen us, and kept out of sight. Not that it matters how he got here. He's here. The question is, where's he going?"

"If he's booked an air passage we can soon answer that," asserted Algy.

"I think we'd better have a look at this," decided Biggles.

"Suppose he sees us?" questioned Ginger.

"I don't see that it matters much. We shan't learn anything by standing here. We must watch what he does. If he sees us—well, maybe that will shake him as much as his arrival here has shaken me. Come on. No—somebody had better stay here to keep an eye on the machines. Bertie, you stay. You may see something from here."

"Look!" cried Ginger. "Is that what he's waiting for?" He pointed to the sky.

Gliding in quietly from the south, apparently preparing to land, was an Auster.

"That's it. That's the answer," replied Biggles crisply. "Smith's in a hurry to see him. The lugger would be some time chugging up the river against the current. Now listen carefully, everybody," he went on. "If that machine collects von Stalhein and takes off again tonight we shall lose track of him. We must stop it somehow. There's only half an hour of daylight left and I doubt if the pilot would risk a night landing on a jungle air strip—if he's going to Daly Flats. Algy, hurry to the control room and ask West, on any pretext he can think of, to keep that Auster grounded for a quarter of an hour; then join Bertie in the Otter. Bertie, stand by to start up. If the Auster *should* leave the ground, follow it, even if it means a night landing when you get back here. Ginger, you come with me. With luck we may get a glimpse of mister mysterious Smith."

By the time they had reached the booking hall the Auster was on the ground, taxi-ing on to the tarmac which, as it happened, was clear of machines. It stopped, but the engine remained ticking over. A man stepped down and waited, looking towards the booking hall. The pilot remained in his seat.

"Do you think that's Smith, waiting by the machine?" asked Ginger.

"No. He looks more like one of these cold-blooded, flat-faced bodyguards, we've seen von Stalhein with before— an Iron-Curtainmonger if ever I saw one. He's here for Erich; we needn't doubt that. Where is he?"

"I saw him in here," answered Ginger, making a beeline for the tea-room.

As they went to open the door von Stalhein came out, so that they met face to face. If he was surprised to see them he did not show it. The only sign of recognition he gave was a curt nod in passing.

"You're in a great hurry," bantered Biggles, turning to follow.

On seeing Biggles almost beside him von Stalhein turned impatiently. "What do you want," he demanded stiffly.

"Nothing—nothing," answered Biggles lightly. "I just wondered who your dour-looking pal was."

"You don't expect me to tell you?"

"Of course not." They were still walking towards the Auster.

"I suppose I have to thank that photograph for bringing you here," muttered von Stalhein savagely.

"Quite right. Naturally, I was interested to see that you were still at the old game. Don't you get tired of playing on the losing side?"

"The game isn't finished yet."

"Yours is, as far as Australia is concerned."

Von Stalhein glanced along the hangars as the Halifax's engines started up. "That, I presume, is Lacey, as busy as ever," he sneered, as, reaching the Auster, he stopped.

"Of course."

"Where's he going?"

"I don't know. That depends on where you go."

Von Stalhein frowned, understanding dawning in his eyes. "So he's going to follow me."

"That's the idea. You can't blame us for taking an interest in your movements."

Von Stalhein hesitated. Ginger could imagine him working out the comparative speeds of the two machines. Actually, there was not much between them.

At this juncture the pilot, a young, good-looking fellow, looked out and stepped into the conversation. "If you want to get home to-night you'd better get in," he said, looking a little worried. "We haven't too much time as it is," he added.

Biggles gave him a quick, appraising glance, as did Ginger, who felt that this was not the sort of remark likely to be made by a member of the gang. Biggles apparently thought this, too, for in a different tone of voice he said: "You can't go yet."

"Why not?"

"Look at the control tower."

The pilot frowned. "But they gave me the okay a minute ago."

"Looks as if they've withdrawn it. There's a Constellation about due in from Singapore."

"Take no notice," ordered von Stalhein harshly, moving towards the cabin. "We must go."

Biggles addressed the pilot. "Your name's Cozens, isn't it?"

"Yes."

"Australian?"

"Yes."

"Full ticket for commercial flying?"

"Yes."

"How long have you had it?"

"Three months."

"How long did it take you to get it?"

"Three years."

"You ignore control tower signals and you'll lose it in three days," Biggles told the pilot seriously.

Von Stalhein's escort, who, with a hand in a side-pocket, had been listening to this conversation with sullen and ill-concealed impatience, broke in, nodding towards Biggles: "Who vas he?"

Answered von Stalhein: "The man I told you about—Bigglesworth."

"So."

"So what," murmured Ginger, well satisfied with the way Biggles's plan for keeping the machine on the ground was working out.

Von Stalhein moved as if to get into the machine.

"I'm sorry, but I daren't leave the ground without an all clear signal," said Cozens, now looking really worried. After all, he was young, and this may have been his first appointment.

"Wise man," complimented Biggles. "It'll be dark in a few minutes, anyway. By the way, I suppose you know the sort of people you're working for?"

"I'm beginning to wonder," rejoined the pilot, looking hard at Biggles.

"Watch your step," advised Biggles.

"Who are you?"

Biggles smiled faintly and indicated von Stalhein. "Ask him—he knows." He glanced at the northern sky. "But here comes the Constellation, so I'll leave you to it. So long." Turning, he walked away.

After a glance at von Stalhein's face, pale with anger, Ginger followed.

"That worked out all right," said Biggles, as they made for the machines. "I don't think the Auster will leave to-night."

"We've shown rather a lot of our hand, haven't we?" asked Ginger anxiously.

"I don't think we've done any harm. Anyhow, there was no other way of keeping them here. I've gained what I wanted—time."

When they reached the machines Algy and Bertie were there. Algy was smiling. "West played up. I was sorry I couldn't see von Stalhein's face when the Auster was refused permission to leave."

Biggles told them what had happened. "Now look, this is the drill," he went on. "Things are about due for a show-down, or they will be if I have my way. I'm going to Sydney in the Halifax, alone, right away. It's close on a two thousand mile run so you needn't expect me back until to-morrow afternoon, however fast I move. If the Auster does take off to-night after all—and West can't hold it indefinitely—there's nothing you can do about it. If it goes in the morning, follow it till it lands, pinpoint the spot, then come back here and wait for me. The place, which I take to be Daly Flats, can't be any great distance away, because working on the daylight factor the Auster could have got there in half an hour or so."

"Is there any likelihood of the Auster *not* going in the morning?" queried Ginger.

"If this fellow Cozens is the right type, and I think he is, von Stalhein and his frosty-faced pal may find themselves grounded. I don't know. We shall see. Keep your eyes skinned for trouble, because knowing you'll follow him, von Stalhein may well try to keep *you* grounded. For the rest, should any unforeseen situation arise you'll have to act on your own discretion. That's all. As soon as the Constellation has cleared I'll press on to Sydney."

91

CHAPTER XII

DISTURBING NEWS

NIGHT, fine and warm, with a moon nearly full and a sky spangled with stars, settled silently over the airport. The beacon held aloft its guiding light. Yellow rays lanced the tarmac from windows of buildings where the duty night-staff worked. Strange aromas, the artificial ones familiar, others strange and sometimes exotic, wafted from time to time to Ginger's nostrils as he squatted on the ground, his back to an undercarriage wheel, watching the scene on first guard.

The Halifax and the Constellation had gone, southward bound. The Auster was no longer in sight. For some time, until darkness dimmed the picture, Cozens and his two passengers had stood by it talking, or, as it seemed to those watching, engaged in argument; possibly, it was thought, discussing the hazards of finding and making a night landing on an unofficial airstrip. At the end Cozens had taxied his machine into a hangar and they had all gone off together. Where they had gone was not known. There had been some talk of shadowing them, but it had not been pursued as there seemed no serious reason for this and Algy preferred to keep his party together. The men, it was agreed, would have to return to the airfield sooner or later to get the machine. In short, it was assumed, naturally, that von Stalhein and his associates had gone to look for a bed for the night and would return in the morning. This may have been von Stalhein's intention but in the event it did not materialise.

About half-past nine Ginger's eyes and muscles were alerted by the silhouette of a man walking quickly from the tarmac towards the Otter. As there was nothing furtive about the approach Ginger's first thought was that it might be West, with news—possibly a radio message from the Halifax. But taking no chances he got up, rapped on the hull—the prearranged warning signal—and awaited the arrival of the visitor.

It turned out to be Cozens, the pilot.

Ginger was astonished, not so much that Cozens should call on them as that he should be allowed to do so; for he could not imagine von Stalhein giving his approval to anything of the sort. It turned out that he had not done so.

"Hello," greeted Cozens.

"Hello yourself," answered Ginger. "You're the last man I expected to see. What can I do for you?"

"You can tell me what your friend meant by that remark of his about watching my step. It's got me worried. This is my first job and I don't want to put a blot on my logbook."

Algy jumped down. "Do your people know you've come here?"

"No."

"So I imagine," said Algy in a queer voice.

"We had a meal. Then I made the excuse of going to make sure that I'd left everything in the machine all right. I had a feeling they didn't want me to talk to you."

"How right you were," murmured Algy.

"They were pretty sore when I refused to ignore the control tower."

"I can believe that. As a matter of interest where did they want you to go?"

Cozens hesitated. "Sorry, but when I was offered this job I gave an undertaking to keep my mouth shut."

"Didn't that strike you as an odd demand?"

"Yes, but beggars can't be choosers. I had nothing to talk about, anyway."

"Well, I won't press you to go back on that if that's how you feel, even though I realise you don't know what sort of crowd you've got mixed up with; but I'll do a deal with you. If I tell you, in strict confidence, why you'd be well-advised to watch your step, will you answer a question for me?"

"That's fair enough."

"Very well. Hold your hat. You're working for an enemy spy outfit."

Cozens's face was a picture. "Did you say *spy* outfit?" His voice cracked with incredulity.

"I did. The real stuff, too. The sort you read about in red-hot thrillers. Cloak and dagger work, with all the trimmings—cyanide pistols, gas guns and what have you."

Cozens clapped a hand to his head. "I must have been

blind," he muttered. "This explains a lot of things."

"Such as landing on Eighty Mile Beach to burn a boat," suggested Algy.

"You know about *that*?"

"Of course. By the way, did you fly an aborigine in to Darwin recently?"

"I did. I wondered what that was for. I don't mind telling you I didn't think much of it."

"Neither did we. It may interest you to know that his job was to set fire to this machine."

Cozens's jaw sagged foolishly. "Who—who are you," he stammered.

"British Security Police."

For a moment Cozens was speechless. Then he blurted: "Stop! I'm in a spin."

"Nothing to the spin you'll be in, old boy, if your pals learn that you've been nattering with us," put in Bertie.

"Are you trying to put the wind up me?"

Algy answered, "No. Just trying to give you an idea of what may happen to you when your employers no longer have any need of your services."

"They wouldn't dare to touch me! I'm an Australian."

Algy smiled sadly. "Listen, chum," he said. "It wouldn't matter if you were King of Australia. When these stiffs have finished with you they'll brush you off like this." He squashed a mosquito that had landed on the back of his hand.

"They're not likely to do that just yet," stated Cozens confidently.

"Why not?"

"Because that'd leave 'em with an aircraft and no one to fly it; and they're in a hurry to get home."

"Where's home?"

Again Cozens hesitated.

"Daly Flats?" suggested Algy.

Cozens started. "Why ask me if you know?"

"We know quite a lot but you could probably fill in some gaps. I advise you to do that, because when this story breaks in the papers your name's going to appear under some ugly headlines."

"Okay," agreed Cozens soberly. "I'll tell you what I know. Then what do I do?"

"That's a ticklish question. It's up to you. Frankly, I think you'd better carry on as you are for the time being and pick up all the information you can. We'll clear you if you get caught in the net when your police get busy. But we're wasting time. Tell us what you know. How long have you been working for this gang?"

"Just on a month."

"What on earth made them employ an Australian pilot—that's what beats me."

"They had another—a foreigner—but he killed himself trying to get into one of these outback landing fields that was too small. I gather they had some urgent business on and had to get a replacement on the spot."

"They'll replace you, I'll warrant, as soon as another arrives from the Iron Curtain," declared Algy grimly. "What have you been doing? Make it snappy. You'd better not stay here too long."

"I've done a lot of flying," volunteered Cozens. "Pretty sticky, some of it, too, landing in out of the way places. Headquarters in the Territory is at Daly Flats. As a result of a radio signal the boss sent me here to pick up a man I didn't know, but who knew I was coming. The other chap came with me to point him out to me—at least, that's what I was told. I'm flying them both to Daly Flats in the morning."

"Who do you call the boss?"

"He goes by the name of Smith. Actually, he's a foreigner, probably a Russian. Anyhow, he talks a lot to Ivan in a language I don't understand, and Ivan's certainly a Russian. He's the fellow with me now. I didn't see anything strange in that because there are plenty of Russians in Australia. Most of 'em are all right."

"Tell me more about Daly Flats."

"It was originally a peanut farm. The man who started it was speared by blacks—they told me that. I believe Smith bought it cheap and cleared a strip so that he could keep in touch with the outside world by air. He certainly does that. The place is miles from anywhere, and the only other way he could get to and fro would be by river, about two miles away. He's got a lugger for dealing with heavy stuff. Oh yes, everything's laid on, radio and so on. Smith has quite an office there. He employs black labour."

"He has other places, I believe."

"Several. That's true, because I've been to some of them."

"Tarracooma, for instance."

"That's right. I was there the other day. Took up a chap from Perth to fix the wireless. Smith says that as a modern pioneer he must keep in touch with his estates. It's the only way in the outback."

"Would you like to make a sketch map for me showing just where this place, Daly Flats, is? It can only be a question of days before the place is raided and that may save us trouble."

"Certainly."

"Then let's go inside. I've pencil and paper there."

"I shall have to be quick. As it is they may be wondering what I'm doing."

"You've left it too late," put in Ginger. "Here they come now. Fasten your safety belts; we're in for a spot of bumpy weather if I know anything."

There was no mistaking the two figures, one burly and the other slim and limping slightly, coming towards the machines.

"Cozens, me lad, I'm afraid you're going to find this a bit difficult—if you know what I mean," observed Bertie.

"Difficult! Why? I'm still doing my job. They can't expect me never to speak to anyone."

"Can't they, by Jove!" answered Bertie warmly. "You don't know these blighters."

"If they start chucking their weight about they'll find I can chuck mine," declared Cozens.

"You still don't seem to understand that you're dealing with people to whom murder is all part of the day's work," Algy told him impatiently. "Get that into your head and never forget it."

There was no time for more, as the two men were almost upon them.

Von Stalhein spoke first. His voice, as cold and brittle as steel, was an indication of his anger, although he did not show it on his face. "So here you are, Cozens. You said you were going to look at the machine."

"So I am. There's plenty of time, isn't there," retorted the pilot.

"You should have told me where you were going."

Cozens flared up. "I like that! Are you telling me who I'm allowed to speak to?"

"While you're in my employ you'll do what you're told. I want to talk to you. Come on."

Cozens looked at von Stalhein. He looked at Algy. Clearly, he was in a quandary. For some seconds there was an uncomfortable silence. Then Algy said: "As presumably they are paying your wages you'd better go with them. We all have to take orders—don't we, von Stalhein?"

Von Stalhein didn't answer. What had upset him, and what he wanted to know, Ginger imagined, was how much Cozens had said. Certainly he had no intention of letting him say any more.

"I suppose you're right," muttered Cozens, answering Algy. "But this being pushed around as if I was a lackey gets my goat. Be seeing you some time." He strode away.

Without another word von Stalhein and his companion followed him.

Algy watched them all go. "What worries me is, Cozens still hasn't grasped the fact that his life is in danger. My only consolation is they're not likely to do anything tonight as they need him to fly them home."

"We shouldn't have let him go," asserted Ginger. "They'll see that he does no more talking, and as soon as they've finished with him he'll disappear."

"We were in no position to stop him," averred Algy. "We set his clock right. The decision was up to him. I know I advised him to go but that was in his own interest. Had he refused, von Stalhein would have known that we'd put him wise, in which case, as he knows too much about them, they certainly would have liquidated him. As it is, von Stalhein has no idea of what was said here so he may hold his hand."

"Don't you think one of us ought to follow them," suggested Ginger.

"I don't think that's necessary. They're bound to stay here till daylight now. We'd do better to get some sleep while we can. I have a feeling that things are going to boil over presently."

Ginger resumed his guard. At midnight, when Algy took over, all was quiet; and so it was when at four o'clock Bertie came on for the dawn watch. Bertie gave the others until six-thirty and then made tea. By the time they had finished a cold breakfast it was broad daylight; but there was still no sign of the Auster's pilot and passengers. The machine remained in its hangar.

"I'd have thought they would have been on the move

by now," said Algy, looking puzzled. "I can't think what could have happened. I hope they haven't pulled a fast one on us."

"I don't see how they could, old boy," opined Bertie. "The Auster is still in its shed."

Eight o'clock came. There was still no sign. Ginger walked over to the hangar and returned to report that the Auster was still there.

By nine o'clock Algy was really worried. "Something's happened. Von Stalhein has given us the slip," he asserted. "And I'll tell you why," he went on. "He knew that if he used the Auster we'd trail it to its hideout."

"The blighter couldn't walk home," averred Bertie, polishing his eyeglass.

"A horrible thought has just occurred to me," said Algy, in an inspired tone of voice. "There's one way he could have got home without walking—or flying. If the *Matilda* brought von Stalhein here, and Biggles considered that possibility, they could have gone off in the lugger. Cozens told us that Daly Flats could be reached by the river."

"If that's the answer we can say good-bye to Cozens," asserted Ginger. "They wouldn't leave him here to come back and talk to us. They'd see him dead first. And if they took him with them it would come to the same thing. They'd never trust him again after what happened last night, and if they didn't need his services to get home they'd have no further use for him. They could get another pilot to collect the Auster when it suited them."

"Here, I say, that's a grim thought," said Bertie. "How far away is this beastly river?"

"The mouth is a hundred miles south-west of here," answered Algy. "I don't know the speed of the lugger and I don't know how far it is up the river to Daly Flats, but if they left here immediately after the row last night, and that's twelve hours ago, they could be on the river by now. Don't forget radio. Von Stalhein might have told Smith what happened here last night and he could have given orders that they were to leave the Auster and come home by the river."

"The next thing we shall hear is that Cozens's body has been found," remarked Ginger gloomily. "We shouldn't have let him go."

"It's no use talking about that now," returned Algy.

"Let's do something. The first thing is to confirm what we suspect. Ginger, slip over to the office, ring the harbour master and ask him if the *Matilda* was in last night."

Ginger hurried off. He was away for twenty minutes and returned at the double. "You were right," he reported briefly. "The *Matilda* came in. It left again just after ten last night."

"In that case I'd say poor Cozens has had it," predicted Bertie, lugubriously.

"He isn't in the town," stated Ginger.

"How do you know that?" asked Algy quickly.

"Because a general order has gone out from Sydney grounding the Auster pending a check on its C. of A.* West had gone off, but the duty officer told me they'd rung up every hotel in the town, looking for Cozens, to warn him that he couldn't leave until lunch-time at the earliest. Biggles must have been responsible for that order. No doubt it struck him as a bright idea to gain time. He wasn't to know that the enemy also had a bright idea, which was to abandon the machine, go home by water, and so give us the slip."

"If the order was issued by Sydney, the Security man Biggles went to see must have had something to do with it," averred Algy. "And his idea, I fancy, was to deprive Smith of his private transport until other orders could be put into effect. It certainly wasn't a coincidence that the Auster had been grounded. Unfortunately it doesn't help us, and it doesn't help Cozens. Incidentally, the order might have been issued to keep him here until Security officers arrived to question him. If that was the scheme it's missed fire. He's gone."

"And gone for good, if I know anything," murmured Bertie.

Algy paced up and down. "This is awful. What are we going to do about it?"

"There's a chance that Cozens may not be dead yet. At least, no one has yet reported finding the body, or we'd have heard of it," remarked Ginger hopefully.

"If he isn't dead he jolly soon will be," declared Algy. "Smith won't be the type to keep a man who's no more use to him. Cozens knows too much for them to let him go."

* Certificate of Airworthiness.

"How about waffling to Daly Flats and giving it a crack—if you see what I mean," suggested Bertie.

"Biggles said we were to be here when he got back," Algy pointed out. "If we go to Daly Flats, and he gets here before we're back, he'll be completely in the dark as to what's happened."

"He also said that if a situation arose we were to act on our own initiative," reminded Ginger.

"You seem to be forgetting that we don't know where this place Daly Flats is!" exclaimed Algy. "That's my fault, and I ought to be kicked," he went on savagely. "Instead of doing so much talking last night when Cozens was here I should have got him to give us the gen right away. He was just going to do it when von Stalhein rolled up. But there, it's easy to be wise after the event. How was I to know that he'd have the brass face to come here?"

"That was a bit of a corker, I must say," conceded Bertie. "It's going to be a ghastly bind sitting here all day doing nothing. Biggles won't be back here for hours. We shall have to do something about Cozens."

"Of course we shall have to do something," cried Algy desperately. "Even supposing he's still alive, which I doubt, he'll be on that lugger. How are we going to get hold of him? Luggers don't have landing decks!"

"We don't know for certain where the lugger is, if it comes to that," contended Ginger. "For a start we could run down to the Daly to confirm that the *Matilda's* on her way up."

"And then what?" requested Algy.

"It'd let the blighters know we're wise to their dirty game," urged Bertie. "If we saw Cozens on deck, still alive, that'd be a load off our minds—if you get what I'm driving at."

"I don't," rejoined Algy bluntly. "What I do see is, if that happened, they'd probably knock him on the head and throw him to the crocodiles. I don't want to be responsible for the man's death."

"We're already responsible for the position he's in, if it comes to that," argued Ginger critically. "The one thing that's quite certain is, we shan't save him by standing here yammering about it."

Algy made up his mind suddenly. "All right," he said. "Let's locate the lugger. Ginger, slip over to the control room and leave word for Biggles about what we're doing in case he gets here before we're back."

Ginger went off at a run.

CHAPTER XIII

DESPERATE MEASURES

THE Otter was soon in the air, heading south-west for the river which, while of no great size as continental rivers go, has a notorious record of death and disaster out of proportion with its length. The ferocity of its native population, its crocodiles and mosquitoes and its sudden spates, combined for years to discourage visitors.

Algy, at the controls, struck the Daly at its broad mouth, where the muddy water meets the sea between slimy banks sometimes fringed with mangroves; for as he had said, they knew neither the speed of the current against which the lugger would have to force a passage, or of the vessel itself. Anyway, seeing nothing of a ship that looked like the lugger on the sea or in the estuary he turned inland.

For ten miles or so there was no break in the flat, reedy shore, often skirted by mudbanks on which crocodiles in startling numbers lay sunning themselves; but thereafter the river began to narrow, winding sometimes between steep, densely-wooded banks. An occasional wisp of smoke revealed the position of a native village or peanut farm. Waterfowl, white herons, pink cranes, black and white jabiru, geese and ducks, stood in the shallows or flighted up and down in clouds of hundreds.

For another twenty minutes, flying low, the Otter droned on at cruising speed. Then Ginger, who was watching ahead, cried: "There she is. At all events that looks like her. I'm afraid they'll have heard us."

"Not necessarily," answered Algy. "They themselves will be making a certain amount of noise. I can't see that it matters much if they do spot us. Well, that settles that question. The *Matilda* is on her way up the river. Now what do we do?"

"Go nearer to see if there's any sign of Cozens."

"Okay."

"You'll have to buck up. The river narrows."

Algy cut the engines. "I'll glide in low. There's a chance we may catch 'em unawares. If Cozens *is* there it should encourage him to know we're keeping an eye on things."

The Otter, nose down, glided on at little more than stalling speed but fast overhauling the lugger.

"There are several people on deck," observed Ginger. "I don't think they've seen us yet. They're looking ahead. That black-bearded ruffian of a skipper is at the wheel. Von Stalhein is with him. Quite a bunch of blacks aft. By gosh! I believe I can see Cozens! Isn't that him sitting on a coil of rope, or something, amidships. Behind the mainmast—with his chin in his hands."

"I think you're right," said Algy tersely. "Yes, that's him. And he's seen us, from the way he jumped up."

"The blacks have seen us, too. They're running forward to tell the skipper."

All faces on deck were now turned upwards, looking at the aircraft, which was still overtaking from about two hundred yards astern and fast losing height."

"If you go any nearer they'll start shooting at us," warned Ginger.

Said Bertie, from behind: "If the dirty dogs start that I've a few things ready to unload on 'em, yes, by Jove!"

"It seems a pity, but I'm afraid we've done all we can do," said Algy helplessly. "Case of so near and yet so far."

No one, either on the ship or in the aircraft, could have been prepared for what happened a moment later. That Cozens himself might do something was a thought that certainly did not enter Ginger's head, for on the face of it he was as helpless as were those in the Otter. Apparently he did not think so. What he did was jump to the rail and dive overboard.

Ginger, remembering the crocodiles, let out a cry of horror.

For a few seconds, Algy, utterly unprepared for such a move, stared unbelievingly; but when Boller raced to the stern of his ship and opened fire with a revolver, blazing shot after shot at the head bobbing in the water, he acted quickly.

What none of those in the aircraft had realised until this moment, although Cozens may have taken it into account, was the speed of the current. Before the *Matilda* had started to turn the swimmer was forty yards astern, with the gap widening rapidly. Others had joined Boller in the stern and bullets were ripping up feathers of water round Cozens's head; but so far apparently none had touched him, for he continued driving on with a powerful overarm stroke. There was really nothing surprising about this, for to hit a moving target the size of a man's head, at long range, with a revolver, would need all the skill of a superlative marksman.

Another factor that Cozens may have considered when he played his desperate stroke was the position of the *Matilda*. The ship, naturally enough, was ploughing its way up the middle of the stream. This meant, as now became evident, that it had the choice of stopping and then going astern, or edging nearer to one of the banks in order to give itself enough room to do a complete turn about at full speed ahead. When Boller had rushed aft the wheel had been taken over by a coloured man, who seemed to be in some doubt as to which course to take. Then, when he did make up his mind and started to turn he found he had insufficient room, and there was some confusion before he succeeded.

All this had occurred in a matter of only two or three minutes, but in that time others had been busy. Cozens still swimming strongly and striking out diagonally for the nearest bank, was now a good two hundred yards away from the lugger, while Algy, after slamming on full throttle and shoving his nose down for speed, had turned on a wing tip, as indeed was necessary if he was not to hit the trees lining the bank—which in fact he nearly did, missing a tall palm by so narrow a margin that Ginger clapped his hands over his face.

The issue was still in doubt, for in order to pick up the fugitive the trickiest part of the flying was yet to come; and there was no time to be lost, for the current that had given Cozens his early advantage was now on the side of the lugger, and it could be only a matter of minutes before the swimmer was overhauled.

Algy did not commit the folly of trying to land downstream on fast flowing water for reasons which need hardly be explained. Apart from anything else, from his position he would have been bound to overshoot his objective by a wide margin, and he would then have been carried on for some distance before he could get round. He took the only practicable course, which was to tear down the river for half a mile, do another vertical turn, and coming back, land in line with the swimmer in order to catch him as he was swept down by the stream. It would, of course, have been impossible for Cozens, no matter how strong a swimmer he might be, to swim against the current.

Algy carried out the first part of the manoeuvre like the experienced pilot he was; but the next step was complicated by the fact that between the machine and the swimmer was a mudbank. As there was no time for the Otter to get down above it before Cozens reached it all Algy could do was land below it, and keeping his nose into the stream, engines running, wait for Cozens to come down to him. So far so good. The position now was the Otter fifty yards below the mudbank, nosing into the fierce current at half throttle, rocking and throwing up a bow-wave, the spray of which, splashing on the windscreen, made it none too easy for those behind it to see what was happening in front. Cozens, coming down fast, was near the upper end of the mudbank and striking out to clear it—Algy, of course, keeping lined up with him. A quarter of a mile away was the *Matilda*, travelling at alarming speed. Ginger prayed fervently that it might run aground on the mud, but Boller must have seen it, too, for in the event this did not happen.

At this stage it struck Ginger that Cozens was doing a lot of unnecessary splashing, considering that all he had to do was float; then, with a strangled gasp of horror he saw the reason. What he had taken to be a pile of dead trees on the mudbank were moving, and he realised they were crocodiles—one of them a grey-green brute nearly twenty feet long. No wonder Cozens was splashing, kicking out again towards the middle of the stream, for any attempt now to reach the river bank must have landed him on the mud amongst the beasts he was striving so desperately to avoid.

Algy, trying to keep in line, was nearly swept down the stream broadside on, but by cutting one engine he managed to straighten out.

Ginger, yelling to Bertie to stand by at the cabin door with a line in case Cozens just missed them, watched in a fever of excitement the swimmer's head bearing down on them, expecting every instant to see it disappear as he was dragged under by the beasts in the water.

Forty yards—twenty—ten. . . . Gasping, Cozens caught the Otter by the bows and hung on, trying to pull himself up. The effort proved beyond him.

"This side," yelled Ginger, making frantic signals.

Cozens let go, clutching at the smooth hull to check his speed. Leaning out, Bertie grabbed him, first by the hair, then under the arms. A heave and a crash and they were both inside, flat on the floor.

Algy waited for no more, but at once started to turn, for the *Matilda* was now so close that he couldn't have got off upstream without colliding with it. Nor, for that matter, could he take off downstream on such a current without risking disaster at a sharp bend a little lower down. But once round he had the legs of the ship, and those on board must have realised it, for the chatter of a machine gun now added to the general frenzy. One or two bullets hit the Otter. Where, Ginger did not know. Like Algy, he was only concerned with getting clear.

The next minute was to live in his mind for ever. He had, in his time, seen some crazy flying; but none like this. As the Otter tore down the river it seemed certain that they would hit something, if not a log or a crocodile then one of the birds which, disturbed by the noise of the engines and machine-gun fire, rose in multitudes from both banks. If the aircraft did not collide with one of them, he thought, it would be due more to the birds than to Algy, who simply had to take his luck. An aeroplane can't dodge birds when they are all around it.

Not until the Otter had secured a lead of a mile did Algy turn into the stream and take off. Airborne, he sideslipped away from a stream of bullets that came up from the lugger, and then pulled up out of range.

"We've done it!" cried Ginger in a thin voice, relaxing in his seat.

Algy, pale of face, smiled wanly. "I can't believe it," he said weakly.

"Where now?"

"Back to Darwin. Better go and see if Cozens is all right."

Ginger went through the bulkhead door to the cabin to find Cozens sitting in a pool of water taking a tot of brandy that Bertie had given him from the medicine cabinet. He looked as if he needed it.

"Are you raving mad, jumping into a river full of crocodiles?" asked Ginger.

"Rather that than stay on a ship manned by a gang of cold-blooded murderers," rasped Cozens viciously.

"Oh, so you discovered that, did you?"

"Yes; but don't you worry, pal; I'll get even with 'em if it's the last thing I do. Pushing me around in my own country with a gun poking in my ribs." Cozens's chief emotion seemed to be anger.

"You can tell us about it presently," said Ginger. "We're making for Darwin."

He returned to the cockpit. "He's all right," he told Algy. "But he seems properly steamed up. On the boil, in fact."

"He's lucky he isn't stone cold," answered Algy, briefly.

Half an hour later, at the airport, Cozens, in borrowed clothes—for his own were of course soaking wet—was telling his story to three attentive listeners. Not that there was much to tell. It appeared that the previous night, as he walked away with von Stalhein and Ivan, even before he had reached the airfield boundary a pistol had been pushed into his back. Finding that protests were useless, and perceiving that his life was hanging on a thread, he had been forced to go to the harbour and on board the *Matilda*, which had at once set sail. The reason why he had not been killed out of hand, he said, was because he had refused to divulge what he had told Algy, and what Algy had told him. This information had been radioed to Smith at Daly Flats. Smith had given orders for him to be taken there so that he could be questioned. He had been told by Boller that Smith would find means to make him speak. "They must have been mighty anxious to know what had passed between us," he concluded. "As you can imagine, I was feeling pretty sick when you blew along in this kite, and as it was obvious that I was to be bumped off anyway it seemed I had nothing to lose by going overboard. I'm a pretty good swimmer, but I don't mind admitting now, in the excitement of seeing you, and in my haste to get off that lugger, for the moment I clean forgot about the crocs. I remembered them all right when I saw them sliding off that mudbank. Not that it would have made any difference. I'd have gone overboard any-way, if only because those swine were sure I wouldn't. We'd seen crocs on the way up. They'd been pointed out to me. The estuary was swarming with the brutes. Pah! Forget it. Thanks for picking me up. I must say that spot of flying was pretty to watch."

"It was hair-raising to be in," alleged Ginger, smiling.

"What are you going to do now," Algy asked Cozens.

"I'm going to Daly Flats, of course," was the staggering reply.

Algy started. "You're *what?*"

"Going to Daly Flats."

"Are you out of your mind?"

"Certainly not. My kit's there. You don't think I'm going to leave that behind, do you? Besides, these crooks owe me a month's pay. They're not getting away with that, either."

Algy looked at the others with an expression of startled despair on his face. "Hark at him!" he said sadly. "The Voice of Young Australia." He turned to Cozens. "We, having been to some trouble to snatch you out of the lions' den, now have the pleasure of watching you leap back into it. Pretty good. How do you reckon to get there?"

"In the Auster, of course."

"You can't. It's grounded. Or it was when we took off this morning."

"We'll see about that," declared Cozens grimly. "Grounded or not, I'm going. At the moment, with hardly anybody there, I've got a chance. When that mob on the lugger arrives I shall have lost it."

"He's got something there, old boy," chipped in Bertie. "That goes for us, too. Now's the time. Now or never, as they say."

Algy shook his head. "This sounds like stark lunacy to me." He looked at Cozens. "What time do you reckon the *Matilda* will get to Daly Flats?"

"About three this afternoon, or soon after."

"As quickly as that?"

"Yes."

"And how long would it take you to get there in the Auster?"

"Half an hour—not more."

107

Bertie looked at Algy. "How about having a smack at it?"

"You mean, go with him?"

"Of course."

"What about Biggles?"

"Someone can stay here with the Otter and tell him all about it. The Auster will take three easily, four if necessary."

"Smith will probably go down to the river to meet the lugger," put in Cozens. "The house is some way from the river. Anyway, that's what I'm gambling on—finding the house empty."

"How many people will be there, not counting Smith?"

"Not more than two or three. Smith's secretary, the cook and a couple of black houseboys who don't count."

"How many on the lugger?"

"Boller, von Stalhein, Ivan, Boller's Malay bosun and eight or nine blacks."

"That would be something to take on," agreed Algy. "Pity Biggles isn't here. This seems to be as good a chance as we shall ever get of looking for that list of agents he's so keen to get hold of."

"And don't forget Cozens knows exactly where the landing strip is," interposed Ginger. "He knows his way about the house. And last but not least, after what's happened, which by this time Smith will have been told about by radio, I imagine, the last thing they'll expect at Daly Flats is the Auster, with Cozens in it."

"I think you're right," agreed Algy. "We'll go and have a look at the place. Ginger, slip over to the office with Cozens and find out what the position is with the Auster."

"That's the stuff," asserted Bertie. "Smite while the jolly old iron's hot. That's me, every time."

Ginger and Cozens went off.

They were not long away, and returned with the information that the order had not yet been cancelled. The duty officer, who knew them through West, who was on night shift, was sympathetic, but could not give the Auster clearance. They could, however, take the machine off at their own risk as long as they were prepared to accept full responsibility, and take the consequences should Sydney make a fuss about it.

Actually, the only man likely to suffer through a breach

of regulations was Cozens, whose licence had been issued in Australia, and could of course be withdrawn by the same authority. It did not take him long to make up his mind, for his blood, as he put it, was up. "Let's get cracking," he said.

Algy looked at his watch. The time was one o'clock. "We have time for a bite of lunch and still be back by the time Biggles gets here," he proposed. After thinking for a moment he went on: "No, we can't all go. Someone will have to stay and tell him what's cooking in case he turns up sooner than expected. Cozens will have to go because he knows the way and has to collect his stuff. Which reminds me: Cozens, you might make that sketch map you spoke about, so that whoever is here will know just where we are."

"That won't take a minute," assented the Auster pilot.

"Now, who stays?" asked Algy, looking round.

"Let's toss for it," suggested Ginger. "Odd man stays."

"Fair enough."

They tossed. Algy lost.

"Tough luck, old boy," sympathised Bertie.

Algy took a spare gun from the magazine and handed it to Cozens. "You'd better put this in your pocket. I've a feeling you may need it."

And he was right.

CHAPTER XIV

GOOD-BYE TO THE AUSTER

In spite of Bertie's carefree attitude towards the projected raid on Daly Flats, Ginger knew that he was well aware of the dangerous nature of the undertaking. That was merely Bertie's way. Ginger himself had no delusions about it. Only Cozens, in spite of his recent experience, seemed genuinely unconcerned. Whether this was due to lack of imagination, or indignation at the treatment accorded him by what he termed "a bunch of Reds," Ginger did not know. The fact remained, he was going to collect his kit with no more qualms than if it had been left in a Darwin hotel instead of at the headquarters of a dangerous organisation that treated lives as mere pawns in its deadly ambition.

Cozens's purpose was to collect his kit and demand the wages due to him. Just that and no more. Ginger didn't know whether to laugh or be angry at this insistence on behaving as though his late employers were ordinary people. With the political angle, Cozens was not in the least concerned. Nor did he appear to be worried by the repercussions that would probably follow the exposure of the spy plot. In a word, with him the matter was a personal one.

The ostensible reason for Ginger and Bertie going with him was to keep him company and perhaps lend him their support—not that he asked for this. And such was the case up to a point. But their real purpose was, of course, to take what seemed to be a unique opportunity of finding out what was going on at Daly Flats, and possibly gather the evidence Biggles needed to close the affair by exposing the spy plot to the Australian authorities.

As a matter of fact it was not until they were on their way, with Cozens at the controls, that Ginger realised that in the pilot himself lay much of the information Biggles wanted. For instance, as a result of flying the so-called Smith about he knew the locations of several outback landing strips apart from Daly Flats and Tarracooma. He had not of course realised the purpose to which these had been put, or where to be put; being an honest man himself he had without question taken Smith's word for it that they were all part of his commercial enterprises. In view of the distances to be covered it sounded reasonable.

Another detail that now emerged concerned the Daly Flats aborigines. According to Cozens they were Arnhem Landers of the worst type. How Smith kept control of them he did not know. There were usually some about, and while not openly hostile they were a surly lot, to say the best of them. They had helped Smith to clear the ground for the airstrip. "I can only think he must dish them out with plenty of grub," said Cozens.

This recalled to Ginger's mind something that had puzzled him, although it had not been discussed. It was

110

this. Knowing about the reputation for unreliability, and, indeed, treachery, held by some of the native tribes, how was it that Smith dare risk deliberately upsetting them? To put it more lucidly, it seemed to him that if, as Biggles supposed, the urging of the natives to revolt and start a sort of Mau-Mau terror in Australia was part of the enemy plan, what guarantee had Smith that they would not turn on him? Did Smith know, and accept, the risks he was running? Or didn't he know? Did he feel able to take care of himself? Was it his intention to escape, by air, when the fuss started? A black had been known to pick up a gun and for no reason at all shoot a white man who had just befriended him. What could you do with people like that, pondered Ginger.

He put the questions to Cozens.

"Don't ask me," replied the pilot. "All I know it, no white man in his right mind would trust some of these black fellas behind him. They don't know what they're doing half the time. People who find excuses for them say they act on impulse. The sight of a gun is enough to make 'em want to shoot somebody and they can't resist the temptation. They don't care who they shoot. I told Smith that, thinking maybe he hadn't been in the country long enough to get the hang of things. In fact, I gave him some newspapers to read, but he only sneered. I know that if trouble does start in these jungles it'll take some stopping. You've only to look down to see what I mean."

Ginger was already looking down, at country very different from what he had seen east of Broome. Here was the real tropical Australia, a dense tangle of trees and palms and towering grasses cut into jig-saw sections by meandering streams. Clearings were few and far between, for Cozens was not following the Daly. Knowing the ground he took a direct course.

After a pause Cozens went on: "Come to think of it there may already be a spot of bother going on."

"What gave you that idea?"

"When I told the traffic manager where I was going he said that if I saw anything of Johnny Bates I could tell him his wife was better. Seems she's been ill."

"Who's Johnny Bates?"

"A police officer. I've never met him. Apparently a black tried to knife somebody the other day and then

111

bolted into the bush. Bates went after him. Been gone a week or more. But that's nothing. When these Northern Territory cops take the trail they keep going till they get their man. Sometimes they're away for weeks—occasionally months—living hand to mouth. Takes some guts, knowing a spear can come at you out of every bush."

"You're telling me," murmured Ginger.

"That's the Fergusson ahead." Cozens indicated a river. "We haven't much farther to go." He altered course slightly, and a few minutes later went on: "That's the place, straight in front."

Ginger regarded with curiosity the establishment about which he had heard so much in a few days. There was no mistaking it for it was the only one in sight, comprising a cluster of corrugated-iron-roofed buildings on one side of an area that had been cleared of bush. Originally intended for planting, this was obviously the landing ground.

His doubts as to the reception they were likely to receive returned. No plan had been made, for it was not possible to make one. As he understood it the procedure was for Cozens to land as if nothing unusual had happened, and going to the house collect his belongings. He would also demand his back pay, either from Smith, or if he were not there, from the clerk. He seemed quite confident that he would succeed in this, but how it would work out in practice was to Ginger a matter for uncomfortable speculation.

As Cozens began a long glide Bertie remarked. "If Smith wanted a place off the map, by Jove, he certainly found it."

"If by that you mean a place well away from white men, you're right," answered Cozens. "But don't fool yourself. There are plenty of blacks down there. They know how to keep out of sight. You could walk about for days and never see one. People who have been into that labyrinth, and were lucky enough to get out, will all tell you that."

Ginger remembered something. "Didn't I once read something about an expedition going into Arnhem Land to look for a white woman who was supposed to have been captured by the blacks—after a shipwreck on the coast, or something?"

"Quite right. The public demanded that something

112

be done about it. An expedition was sent but it found nothing, as the old-timers prophesied. They heard whistles and saw smoke signals—that was all. When a black goes into hiding a white man's wasting his time looking for him."

By this time the Auster was coming round for its approach run.

"Are you going straight down?" asked Ginger.

"Sure I am. No use fiddling about."

"I can't see a bally soul," said Bertie.

"The people in the house may not have heard us—but from the scrub plenty of eyes will be watching us."

No more was said. Cozens made a neat landing, finishing his run near the house. "Are you fellows coming with me?" he asked, as he switched off and prepared to get down.

"Of course," answered Ginger. "We can keep an eye on the machine from the house. There's not likely to be anyone here able to run off with it, anyway."

They all got down.

"The door's open," observed Cozens. "They must have heard us by now. Queer there's nobody about. Smith will probably have gone to the river to meet the lugger."

The word queer, Ginger thought, was the right one. Even allowing for the drone of the engine that had for some time filled their ears, the silence that hung over the place was unnatural. The air was heavy. The heat was sultry, with rank unhealthy smells. The whole atmosphere, he felt, as his eyes made a swift reconnaissance, was sombre with a foreboding of evil. A sensation crept over him as of waiting for a bomb to explode.

Even Cozens seemed to be aware of this, for he, too, looked around with a puzzled frown lining his forehead. "There's something phoney about this," he said. "I don't like it."

"What don't you like?" inquired Ginger.

"The absence of the blacks. That's a bad sign. There were always some about whenever I've been here."

"You think they've gone?"

"Not likely. They're watching us."

"Here, have a heart, laddie," protested Bertie. "You're giving me the creeps."

"Keep your eyes skinned," warned Cozens.

Ginger pointed. "Isn't that somebody lying on the
113

ground over there, by that shed? Looks like a black."

They walked towards the object. It was a black. He was lying flat. He was lying flat because he was dead.

"He was one of the houseboys," said Cozens. "I remember his face."

"There's another over there," said Bertie.

They didn't go to the second body, which was lying near some scrub. It was, Cozens averred, too near cover, and within easy spear-throw of it. "Let's get to the house," he said shortly.

Keeping close together they walked towards the door.

At a distance of a few yards Cozens stopped abruptly, staring at something on the ground, just inside.

The others stopped. They, too, stared at what he had seen.

It was a foot—or rather, a boot. A leather boot.

With slow deliberation Cozens took out his gun. Holding it at the ready he advanced. On the threshold he stopped again. They all stopped.

On the floor lay the dead body of a man. A white man. In uniform.

Cozens, pale as death himself, drew a deep breath. "Bates," he said. "That's who it'll be, Bates." Swiftly his eyes explored every corner that might conceal the murderer.

"How awful," was all Ginger could say.

"He must have followed his man here."

Bertie stooped beside the body of the dead policeman. "Shot," he announced. "Shot in the head, from behind. Where's his gun?"

"They must have taken it."

"We were just too late," said Bertie. "He can't have been dead for more than half an hour."

"But surely the people in the house wouldn't have been so mad as to shoot a policeman," opined Ginger.

"No. Bates was after his man. The man ran in here. Bates followed him. He was shot from behind. There might have been more than one black. When the shooting started the house boys bolted. Who killed them I can't imagine. It doesn't matter. We'd better get out of this. It may have stirred up a hornet's nest. Every black on the place will be on the jump. We'll take Bates with us."

"But what about the white people in the house," asked

Ginger, beginning to recover from the shock of their terrible discovery.

"They may have bolted. Let's see."

It was soon ascertained that they hadn't bolted. They were dead, killed by spear thrusts; the clerk in his office, the cook in the kitchen and another houseboy in a passage. Everywhere things had been smashed, or lay about in disorder.

"They must still have been at it when they heard us coming," said Cozens. "What a shambles."

"And only on the way here we said it was the sort of thing that might happen," muttered Ginger. "What do you suppose could have started them off?"

"Bates. He was after one of them. They killed him, and the sight of blood was all that was necessary to send them crazy. They're like that. Come on. The sooner we get word of this to Darwin the better. Be ready to shoot fast. They'll be watching. They may do nothing, but they may come for us. If they do, and get between us and the machine, we've had it."

Instinctively Ginger walked to the door to look at the aircraft. Near it lay what appeared to be a dead tree stump. It looked natural enough, with broken ends of branches protruding; but what puzzled him was he couldn't remember seeing it before. This was all the more astonishing because it was dead in front of the Auster, which, had it run on a little farther must have collided with it. Cozens, Ginger was sure, would never have taken such a risk had the stump been there.

Had it been there? He stared; but the stump looked as dead as a lump of rock. Turning, he called the others. "There's something here I don't understand," he said. "Cozens, did you nearly run into a tree stump when you landed?"

"Tree stump?" echoed Cozens, hurrying forward.

Ginger turned back. "Yes," he answered. "There's a——" The words died on his lips, for there were now two stumps.

Cozens took one comprehensive look. Raising his gun he began slowly to advance, at the same time saying: "Stumps my foot. That's two of 'em. Watch out for spears."

Even though he had been warned Ginger was unprepared for the speed at which the stumps came to life. In a flash they were erect, and two spears were on their way.

The white men ducked or jumped clear, and the spears buried their points in the wooden wall of the house with a crisp double thud. Having thrown, the two blacks fled in great leaps. Cozens fired. One fell, but he was on his feet again in an instant, and with his fellow disappeared in the jungle.

"Let's go," said Cozens, briskly. "There may be scores of them. Keep close. Cover me while I get in. While I'm getting started up blaze away on both sides."

"What about Bates," asked Ginger.

"We shall have to leave him. It's going to take us all our time to get aboard without anything to carry."

The truth of this was soon apparent, for as they moved forward a score of blacks burst from the bushes and in a moment the air was full of spears. Several blacks raced to get between the aircraft and the white men.

"Back," yelled Cozens. "Back to the house. It's no use. We can't do it."

There was a rush to get back to the door, everyone taking it in turns to shoot while the others retired. It was not exactly a dignified withdrawal, but it was at least successful. To Ginger it seemed like a miracle that none of them had been struck. Spears stuck in the ground along their path.

Panting, inside, they looked at each other.

"Let's rattle 'em from the windows," said Bertie. "By Jove! I must say that was a bit of a do."

As they took up positions at the windows a strangled cry broke from Ginger's lips.

There was no need for him to explain.

The Auster was on fire.

CHAPTER XV

THE BATTLE OF DALY FLATS

FOR a minute or two those in the house could only watch
with helpless resignation and dumb despair the destruction
of the Auster. There was no question of trying to save it
even if the blacks had not been there, for one of the
spears, with a flaming brand attached, that had been used
to fire it had pierced a fuel tank with a result that need
not be described. The heat had driven back the blacks,
but they were still there, doing a follow-my-leader dance
in close procession, shaking their spears, yelling, and
stamping on the dry earth until the dust flew. Even one
who had been wounded joined in, limping as he staggered
round. Another lay still. His companions paid no attention
to him.

The only consolation Ginger could find in the disaster
was that the blacks had occupied themselves with a war
dance instead of attacking the house immediately. They
were at least being given a respite.

Cozens took aim with his gun, only to lower it with an
exclamation of disgust. "Pah! What's the use. The
damage has been done."

"Pity this couldn't have happened when that stinker
Smith was here," remarked Bertie, wiping condensation
from his eyeglass.

"It could have done," answered Cozens moodily. "It
isn't us in particular that they're mad to kill. Anyone
would do. It just happened that we rolled up at the worst
possible moment. In another hour, when they'd let off
steam and realised what they'd done, they would probably
have bolted into the bush. We caught them on the boil."

"What will they do next?" asked Ginger.

"I don't suppose they know themselves. They may have
a go at us, or, when the frenzy has worn off, fade away."

"Thank goodness the house has got a tin roof or they
might have tried spearing that with their beastly fire-
works," observed Bertie.

Said Cozens: "While we're waiting for them to make up their minds what they're going to do we'd better tidy up. We can't leave these bodies lying about. You keep your eye on 'em, Ginger, and yell if they come for us."

Cozens and Bertie went off, and leaving Ginger on guard at the window. They were away about ten minutes. "What are they doing?" asked Cozens, when they returned.

"They're gone," Ginger was able to tell him. "They went into a huddle and then walked away into the bushes."

"Hm." Cozens considered the prospect. "They may be cooling off or they may be planning a trick. They know plenty. Shoot at anything that moves, even if it looks like an animal. How goes the time?"

Ginger glanced at his watch. "Quarter to three. Biggles might get back to Darwin any time now. When we fail to show up he'll come along in the Otter to find out what's happened."

"That'll be dandy and no mistake," said Bertie. "He'll step right into the custard."

"We'll have to warn him to keep clear."

"How?"

"I wonder could I get Darwin on the radio. There's one here, or should be."

"You mean there was one," rejoined Bertie. "The bright boys outside have made it look like a cat's breakfast. The blighters aren't so dumb that they don't know about radio."

"In that case we shall have to think of something else," said Ginger.

Silence fell. The heat was awful. Outside, nothing moved except the smoke still rising into the sultry air from the smouldering remains of the aircraft. Had it not been for that Ginger would have found it hard to believe that this horror had really happened—in a country he had always imagined to be as safe as England. But then, he reflected, the people in Kenya must have felt like that before the Mau-Mau trouble started.

"Twenty past three," said Bertie. "What about Smith, and that bunch on the lugger? According to you, Cozens, they should soon be here."

"If they come, they're likely to walk right into it, too."

"Best thing that could happen, absolutely," declared Bertie. "It'd tickle me to death to see that swine Smith on the end of a spear. Serve the blighter right. He was responsible for this beastly mess."

Outside, all remained quiet.

"Do you think they've gone?" asked Ginger.

Cozens shook his head. "No. They're probably skulking in the scrub, watching for one of us to go out. Time means nothing to them. They might keep it up for days."

"How jolly!" murmured Bertie.

"I was wondering about putting out a warning signal for Biggles," explained Ginger. "He'll come, and I'm scared stiff he'll land."

"My advice is, wait till you hear him," replied Cozens. "At present the blacks must think they've got us cornered. When they hear another machine coming they may think twice, and push off."

Ginger looked at Bertie. "While we're doing nothing we might have a look round Smith's office to see what he's been up to. That was really why we came here."

"That's an idea," agreed Bertie. "This waiting is binding me rigid."

They found plenty of papers in Smith's office, some of them on the floor, for the natives appeared to have enjoyed making as much mess as possible; but all written matter was in code or in a language neither Ginger nor Bertie could read. They took it to be Russian.

"The back-room boys will be able to sort this out," predicted Ginger.

"If we can get it to them, which at the moment appears to present difficulties, old boy—if you see what I mean."

"What's in here, I wonder," went on Ginger, going over to a closed door. It was locked. He called to Cozens: "What's in this room leading off Smith's office?"

Cozens replied: "I don't know. I was never allowed to see inside it. It was always kept locked."

"Let's unlock it," suggested Bertie, putting a foot against the lock and throwing his weight on it.

For a moment the door held, but when Ginger added his weight it flew open with a splintering crash.

"Well, blow me down!" ejaculated Bertie, looking round.

The room appeared to be both an armoury and a chemist's shop. Guns and rifles stood in racks with boxes of ammunition at their feet. On a bench were instruments, scales, bottles of chemicals, racks of test tubes and retorts.

On a table was a pile of what seemed to be pieces of rock.

"Smith wasn't going to run short of weapons," observed Bertie.

"He could never have intended to use all these," declared Ginger. "A lot of it is cheap stuff, obsolete. I'd say the idea was to dish it out to the blacks when the time was ripe. That's it," he went on confidently. "And I'll tell you something else. I'd bet it was this sort of stuff that von Stalhein's ship was bringing here when it struck the willie-willie and went aground on the island. They'd never have got it through Customs. It would have been unloaded on the lugger and brought up the river. It all fits."

"That's about the English of it, laddie," agreed Bertie. "What's all this junk on the table?"

"Mineral specimens. Couldn't be anything else. Smith, or one of his men, has been prospecting, probably for uranium. There have been some big finds in Australia. We found a Geiger Counter on the island. Now we know what it was for. The ship carried money, too; perhaps to pay the natives, in which case it will most likely turn out to be phoney."

"Absolutely," confirmed Bertie. "Those are the answers. What have we here?" He lifted the lid of a box. "Bombs! by Jingo. He was all ready for the blacks if they turned on him. No, these aren't ordinary grenades. They're tear-gas. The blighter thought of everything."

"They may come in useful," said Ginger thoughtfully.

They went back to Cozens, who was cautiously opening a window. "I'm letting in some air," he told them. "This heat is killing me. This is the sort of sticky heat you get here when the wet is on the way; but it isn't due for another week or so."

"What's the wet?" asked Ginger.

"The rains. You haven't seen it rain till you've seen it raining here. It buckets down, and it keeps on bucketing. Maybe that's what's affecting the blacks. It gets on everyone's nerves. I'll tell you this; if we don't get out of here before it starts we're likely to be here for some time. With visibility nil there's no question of a plane coming for us."

"You're a bright and breezy bloke," remarked Bertie. "Think of something else to cheer us up."

Cozens looked critically at the sky. "I don't like the

look of that glare. Something's going to happen. How goes the time?"

"Quarter to four," answered Ginger. "If Biggles——" Cozens stopped him by holding up a hand. "Listen!"

At last the silence outside was broken. It was broken by the sound of voices, still some distance off, but approaching.

"That's Smith's party," asserted Cozens. "I know his voice. He always talks as if everyone was deaf. Looks as if he may get caught in his own trap. We shall soon see."

"We can't let him do that," objected Ginger.

"Why not?"

"There's something not nice about standing by doing nothing while white people are speared by blacks."

"That's pretty good," sneered Cozens. "Why, according to you he's the very man who's here to rouse the blacks against the whites. He's roused 'em. Okay. Now let the skunk see what a good job he's made of it. I'm not forgetting Johnny Bates, in the next room."

"There's nothing we can do, anyway," put in Bertie.

"Of course there isn't," argued Cozens. "You fellers can do what you like, but I'm not risking a spear in my neck to save a thug who would have bumped me off, and who's about due for hanging, anyway."

"We could at least shout, to give them a chance," suggested Ginger.

"Okay. Shout if you like. But if it happens that the blacks have gone you'll see what Smith'll do to us—if he can."

Ginger went to the window. "Von Stalhein," he shouted.

"That's the way from the river. There's a track, over there," said Cozens, pointing.

"Von Stalhein," yelled Ginger.

The voices stopped. Silence fell. Beads of sweat trickled down Ginger's face. "Go back," he shouted. "The blacks are on the warpath."

The warning did not achieve its object. What happened would probably have happened in any case. Ginger's shout may merely have expedited things. Smith, actuated more by curiosity than fear, did the most natural thing, as might have been expected.

"There he is. That's Smith," said Cozens, as a heavily built man appeared from the path he had pointed out. With him was Ivan, another white man, and two blacks carrying parcels. They hurried forward, looking about them, apparently for the owner of the voice that had called.

Ginger watched for the crew of the lugger to appear—and, of course, von Stalhein. However, they had not shown up by the time the storm broke.

On seeing the burnt out remains of the aircraft Smith stopped, pointed, said something to the others and hastened towards it. The two natives put down their parcels and waited. There was not a movement in the jungle and Ginger decided that the blacks must have gone.

But Cozens must have seen something that aroused his suspicions; or it may have been the very absence of movement that told him what was about to happen; at all events, from the open door towards which they had all moved, he suddenly shouted: "Look out!"

He was too late. In an instant the air was full of flying spears, thrown by blacks who had appeared from nowhere, as the saying is."

Ivan and his companion, being behind Smith, fell at once. They hadn't a chance even to draw their guns. Smith ran towards the house.

By this time those in the doorway were shooting; two or three blacks fell, and it may have been as a result of this that Smith got as far as he did. With only ten yards to go he sprawled forward with a spear between his shoulder blades, hurled by a black who had raced after him. Ginger could see what was going to happen; but Smith and the black were in line, and none of them dare shoot for fear of hitting the wrong man. As Smith collapsed the black also went down, hit perhaps by three bullets, for everyone fired at him.

Of the two natives who had been carrying the parcels, one turned at the first indication of trouble and fled up the path, never to be seen again. The other made for the house and succeeded in reaching it with a spear trailing from his thigh. He fell inside, gasping.

The main body of blacks were now busy retrieving their weapons, regardless of the sniping that continued from the doorway. At this juncture Ginger remembered something. The tear-gas bombs. Dashing to the box he filled his pockets and returned with one in each hand. Running into the open he threw them all in quick succession as far as he could. What effect they had could not be discerned, for the blacks were enveloped in the fast-spreading white vapour of the gas. He turned back to the house to see Cozens and Bertie trying to carry Smith into the house, not very successfully, for he was a heavy man, and the spear got in the way. Cozens, ashen, pulled it out, and then said it was no use. The man was already dead. The spear had reached his heart.

As if affairs were not sufficiently hectic more confusion was now caused by the drone of a plane, and looking up Ginger saw the Otter burst into view, flying low over the treetops.

"Here's Biggles," he cried. "Are we going to let him land?"

Actually, they had no say in the matter, for the Otter's wheels were down and it was already coming in.

"Let's throw some more gas," shouted Cozens. "Where did you get it?"

Ginger told him, and a rush was made for the box. A minute later all three of them were hurling bombs into the scrub into which the blacks had withdrawn. That the gas was having the desired effect was made clear by the uproar in the bushes.

By now the Otter was on the ground. It rolled to a stop thirty yards away and men began to jump down. First out was Biggles, pale and red-eyed from want of sleep. He did not look too pleased as he snapped: "What on earth's going on here?"

"The blacks have gone mad," Ginger told him tersely. "Hark at 'em! They've killed I don't know how many people. We've just driven them back with Smith's tear-gas grenades."

"Where is Smith?"

Ginger pointed. "There he is. Dead. Speared."

Bertie and Cozens came up. From the other side came four men unknown to Ginger. Algy stood by the machine.

Biggles made some brief introductions. The newcomers turned out to be Colonel MacEwan, the Security Officer, and his personal assistant, and two police officials.

"Who started all this?" Biggles, looking worried, wanted to know. "Algy told us what happened last night and this morning, and why you came on here."

"We didn't start it you may be sure," answered Ginger vehemently. "It had started when we got here. Bates, the policeman from Darwin, had been murdered, and so had everyone else in the house. We walked right into it, and got to the house by the skin of our teeth, whereupon the blacks set fire to the Auster."

Ginger, Cozens and Bertie then took turns to narrate in more detail the sequence of events.

"How many blacks are there in this mob?" inquired Colonel MacEwan, nodding towards the jungle, now silent.

"There's about a score left," answered Cozens.

"We should be able to handle them if they come back, which I doubt," replied the Colonel. "Now we'll have a look at things."

From this point the Australian authorities took over.

"I waited at Darwin for a bit, for you to come back," Biggles told Ginger and Bertie, Cozens having gone to the house with his superiors. "When you didn't show up I guessed you'd come unstuck and pressed on to see what had happened. This place was due to be raided, anyway. That's why Colonel MacEwan came back with me. By the way, where's von Stalhein?"

"He isn't here," informed Ginger. "I don't think any of the people on the lugger came back with Smith from the river. Maybe there was a row about Cozens escaping. I don't know."

Biggles nodded. "Von Stalhein need talk of *our* luck. He usually manages to slip away when Old Man Death's about. No matter. The police will pick up the lugger, no doubt, when it tries to get out of the river—if not before."

It may be said here that this did not happen, in spite of strenuous efforts to catch the *Matilda*. What saved it was the early arrival of the "wet", which destroyed visibility for days and must have given the lugger a lucky chance to slip out of the river undetected. Ginger, remembering Smith's native servant who had bolted back down the path when the blacks had attacked, thought this man must have reached the river and given the alarm. At all events, his body was not found in the general clean-up. Some weeks later, wreckage thrown up on one of the Melville Islands was believed to be that of the lugger. But this was not proved, and the police are still on the lookout for Boller and his crew.

* * *

There is little more to be said. It was only necessary for Colonel MacEwan to walk through the house to satisfy himself of the truth of Biggles's allegations. The Otter went at once to Darwin with a mass of papers, and returned, with the Halifax, bringing a force of police sufficient to prevent any further interference on the part of the blacks, who, as a matter of detail, when sanity returned must have realised what they had done, for they quietly faded away into their jungle retreats.

Papers revealing the names of enemy agents operating in Australia, including those who had landed in the lifeboat with von Stalhein, were found, and the entire plot exposed, although for security reasons the soft pedal was kept on the story. The black servant who had reached the house with a spear in his thigh recovered, and gave some valuable evidence.

The scheme was much as it had been visualised. The plan was to spread a network of agents and operatives all over the continent both to spy on secret experimental work with atomic and guided missiles, and undermine the country's economy by the infiltration of agitators into the native settlements as had been done elsewhere. When the trouble started certain selected blacks were to be provided with firearms. Behind the background of disorder scientists were to explore the outback for minerals useful in nuclear research. It was some of these people, with their weapons and equipment, who were on board the ship which was to have met the *Matilda* by appointment, and transferring to it, gone on up the Daly. It was not a matter of bad luck that this failed. Someone blundered in attempting to do it not only in the season of willie-willies, which in North-West Australia can occur at any moment between November and April, but in the most notorious zone of all, between Exmouth Gulf and Eighty Mile Beach.

Biggles and his party returned to Darwin at sundown having handed over to Colonel MacEwan. They never saw Daly Flats again, having no reason, and certainly no desire, to do so. After a rest, during which time Biggles made a full report of his part of the affair for the authorities, they paid a courtesy visit to Bill Gilson at Broome, and then made a leisurely run back to London. They learned later that Bill had received promotion for his handling of the Tarracooma business, which resulted in long prison sentences for his prisoners.

Cozens soon got another job and is now flying a Qantas Constellation. Not only was no action taken over his violation of the regulations with regard to the Auster, which, as had been supposed, Biggles had caused to be grounded, but in view of the part he had played, he was awarded compensation for what he had lost.

So taking things all round, the only people who came to any harm from Biggles's visit to Australia were those whose sinister conspiracy had taken him there.

Which was as it should be.

From Alfred Hitchcock,
Master of Mystery and Suspense—

A thrilling series of detection and adventure. Meet The
Three Investigators – Jupiter Jones, Peter Crenshaw and Bob
Andrews. Their motto, "We Investigate Anything", leads
the boys into some extraordinary situations – even Jupiter's
formidable brain-power is sometimes stumped by the bizarre
crimes and weird villains they encounter. But with the
occasional piece of advice from The Master himself, The
Three Investigators solve a whole lot of sensational mysteries.

Armada

has a whole shipload of exciting books for you

Armadas are chosen by children all over the world. They're designed to fit your pocket, and your pocket money too. They're colourful, exciting, and there are hundreds of titles to choose from. Armada has something for everyone:

Mystery and adventure series to collect, with favourite characters and authors . . . like Alfred Hitchcock and The Three Investigators – the Hardy Boys – young detective Nancy Drew – the intrepid Lone Piners – Biggles – the rascally William – and others.

Hair-raising Spinechillers – Ghost, Monster and Science Fiction stories. Fascinating quiz and puzzle books. Exciting hobby books. Lots of hilarious fun books. Many famous stories. Thrilling pony adventures. Popular school stories – and many more.

You can build up your own Armada collection – and new Armadas are published every month, so look out for the latest additions to the Captain's cargo.

Armadas are available in bookshops and newsagents.

Armada